Robbie

and the Agents of

Corliol

Michael Manley

First Edition: *Robbie and the Agents of Corliol* by Michael Manley

ISBN: 978 1 9173650 2 4

First published in the UK in 2024 by Caldew Press.

Caldew Press
Tolivar
12 St George's Crescent
Carlisle
CA3 9NL

www.caldewpress.com

Printed in Great Britain by Amazon.

CALDEW PRESS

To
Stan and Marjorie
Reunited

Acknowledgements

Heartfelt thanks to:
All who supported me through a trying time and continue to do so.

In particular those who gave me sanctuary to write:
my generous family,
and
Mark and Mandy,
Jan and John,
Pete and Chrissie,
Geoff and Elizabeth,
Alex, Hazel, Theodore and Lucia,
Brian and Lesley,
Chris and Geraldine.

To my wise and gracious mentor Helen Weston.

To the loving people of Cumbria, especially their inspiring young people.

To Phil Hewitson and all at Caldew Press.

The City of Corliol and the World of Shallowness is a fantasy.

Any resemblance to real persons or other real-life entities is purely coincidental. All characters and other entities appearing in this work are fictitious. Any resemblance to real persons, dead or alive, or other real-life entities, past or present, is purely coincidental.

No animals were harmed in the production of this work.

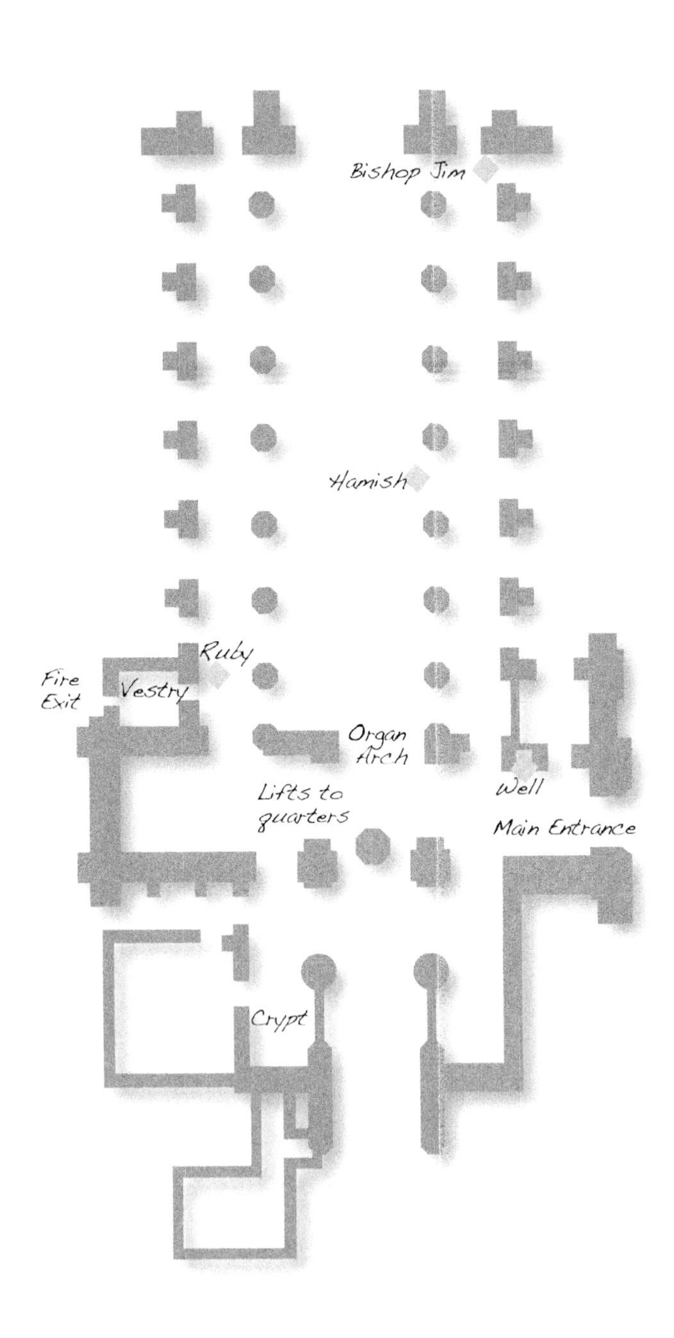
Bishop Jim
Hamish
Ruby
Fire Exit
Vestry
Organ Arch
Lifts to quarters
Well
Main Entrance
Crypt

CHAPTER 1 — ROBBIE DISINTEGRATES

Robbie froze, in both senses of the word. First, he could not move. Second, an icy chill invaded his body dismissing his thick camouflage jacket and combat trousers. He just stood there, gulping short, sharp, breaths. His stomach twisted tortuously; his legs wobbled rhythmically, and his lungs burned as if at the end of a cross-country run. In desperation he gripped his thumping chest, then rushed his trembling hands to cushion his exploding temples: but it was all in vain. He had nothing more to give. *Was this dying?*

Sinking to his knees on the cold stone pavement, he sealed his flooding eyes. Why had he ever agreed to get involved? Why couldn't he have said no? Why hadn't he noticed her? It was all his fault.

CHAPTER 2 — THE OMINOUS NIGHT BEFORE

Robbie was a stargazer and loved the night sky. Tonight, he had scaled the heavy cathedral gates easily and sat astride them victoriously, catching his breath. He pulled out his extendable brass telescope and surveyed the grounds like a general on a steed surveying his battlefield. He had only been caught once before in the cathedral precinct, but that night he had sneaked in much earlier, and been rewarded richly – not just spotting *The Plough* (or *Big Dipper* as some called it) but also *Ursa Major! (The Great Bear)* a sparkling *dot-to-dot* in the heavens. He'd then been spotted by one of the vicars (or canons as they were called) and had to scarper quickly. Tonight though, was his.

The great doors were locked and the tall arches, sealed with kaleidoscope glass, were masked in darkness – perfect for stargazing. Robbie swung his leg over, lowered his lithe eleven and a half year old body down as far as he could, and then let go – crunch. He crouched on the tarmac, attentively squinting left and right, but not even the shadows were moving. He smiled. It promised to be a great night.

Unfortunately, that turned out to be his first mistake.

Robbie's quest for darkness had often taken him into these sleeping grounds, but at this later hour, something was different, something was wrong, or not quite right. It was then that he heard it. A bizarre, dreamy, high pitched, theremin-like chanting seeping through the cathedral stone. He tip-toed nearer. *Yes, definitely singing, definitely high pitched and definitely WEIRD! Who on earth would be in the cathedral in the early hours of the morning? And what's more, what on earth were they doing?*

He stepped back and spotted the stars on the ceiling shimmering in a strange light, casting shadows on the decorative shields and painted figures of angels resting on its beams. Something was definitely not right.

He considered returning to the gates to gain a vantage point but then chanced on a tree, its higher branches more level with the windows. Tucking his telescope inside his jacket, he began to climb. The first two branches were a cinch, but the third proved more difficult. *Come on, come on, you can do it,* he told himself as he dug his army boot into the trunk and stretched above him. The wood began to graze his palms, and he realised just how high he was going, and worryingly, just how easy it would be to fall!

The stench of pigeon waste filled his nostrils; his mouth dried; but he managed to grab the limb overhead. He held on tight, hanging precariously like an inexperienced sloth, as he wondered what to do next. *Only one thing for it*, he thought, as he swivelled a leg over, then, laying on his stomach, hugged the branch in trepidation. His breath was racing, his hands were shaking – he hated climbing trees!

He caught his breath, then shuffled forwards, sighing in relief as the bough held his weight. The bark, however, scratched into his commando trousers, burning the top of his legs. *Ow.* He wasn't confident enough to stand, but bravely pushed his weight through his arms, stepping his hands towards him until he was in an upright position. *Phew*. Next, with one hand secured to the branch, he gingerly let the other feel for his scope and retrieve it. Then it hit him! *How, with only one hand, was he going to pull out the sections in order to see?* 'Damn,' he moaned.

Taking a deep breath, he tentatively released his steadying arm and gently held it out, like a tight-rope artiste, to see if he could balance, his thighs fearfully glued to the branch. *So far so good!* He sighed. Then he slowly and deliberately placed his hand on the lens and delicately extracted first one section, then the other. He exhaled with relief, his fringe now dripping with sweat as he immediately shot his hand back to the safety of the branch.

He raised his scope to his eye, but it was out of focus! *Typical!* He would have to repeat the whole dreadful escapade all over again! In some ways, he later wished he hadn't; for turn by turn, he was not prepared for the stupefying scene that unfolded.

His mouth dropped open; his eyes blinked in disbelief: for there before him was something more mystifying than the stars, more incredible than a black hole! Though there wasn't a soul in there, there was something much, much worse! Not a person, but a bunch of what looked like mice, ON THEIR HIND LEGS, processing reverently into the canons' seats! *Mice? On hind legs?* He gasped. On top of that, there was something even more disturbing. These so-called mice were dressed in miniature canons' coats and had unnatural human-like faces!

Robbie nearly lost his balance. *Impossible!* he gulped.

Straining as far forward as he dared, he still couldn't work out what they were singing: yet in an uncanny way the melody seemed to calm his mind and rest his heart.

He zoomed in on a female with purple meringue-like hair, who seemed to be conducting.

#

Inside the cathedral, the rodent night-shift canons (known as guardians), continued their song.

Guardians of the Temple Courts, listen one and all, hush your minds, breathe in, let go; hear the Maker's call.

Alison, the choir mistress, was in heaven. With a music score in one hand, she raised and lowered the other like a trawler traversing invisible waves.

Suddenly a great *thud*, followed by a metal clatter, broke the serenity. Guardian Harold, complete with fogged-up flying goggles, had clumsily crashed his chairicopter – a curious cross between a hand-pedalled recliner bike and a helicopter – onto his stall. (Yet again he had overdone the pedalling on the way up and under-compensated on the way down.) At the commotion Guardian Petunia, the most delicate of the community, seized her lilac cardigan and dutifully fainted. Robinson, the gentle giant and her neighbour, skilfully caught her, then gently laid her down, fanning her until she came around.

Ben and Sam, the youngest guardians, in the stalls opposite, covered their mouths trying not to laugh. It wouldn't have mattered if they did, because the twins were both deaf and mute. This had never held them back, however, Ben enjoyed wild swimming and scuba-diving and Sam loved skateboarding and BMX. They had only been accepted into the community because Guardian

Brian, the novice master, had argued that guardianship was not based on what you could do, but on the Maker's call, which, in his view, both had clearly experienced. (The community had agreed and came to appreciate the beautiful way they signed the chants.)

Harold eventually recovered, bowing in apology to Marcus, the Prior, but as Harold opened his mouth to sing, the chant ended.

The guardians sat and settled.

Every eye then turned to face Hamish, the brass eagle: well, not every eye, because Guardian William, an ex-marine sniper, only had one eye that worked. He'd lost the other in the Great Feline war of '99, when his crossbow had backfired and he'd been invalided out – though he'd argued that with one eye permanently closed, he was a better shot than before.

'The first lesson is te'ken from the first book o'Kings,' the eagle began, in a pensive Highland accent.

'Oh, I wish he'd get on with it,' whispered Edmund, the guardian responsible for organising the worship, 'Why does he always make a meal of it?'

Harold, who sat next to him, smiled, but said nothing.

Hamish continued: 'The nineteenth chapter beginning at the ninth verse.'

Edmund couldn't help but yawn. He looked along his row. Like the daytime canons, each guardian was allotted a numbered stall. On his side were even numbers, on the other, odd.

Alison, stall VIII, sat to his left. Next came Ben and Sam (each wearing a Corliol United scarf), who were distracted as usual: perched on the edge of their stalls swinging their legs and signing to one another surreptitiously.

Then it was Petunia and Robinson and finally, Brian.

Across from him snoozed Molly, the engineer (who had apparently been up all day servicing the fridges).

Then Gustav, the chef: twiddling his handlebar *mouse-stache*.

Then sadly an Empty stall, number XV, which still bore a posey of hopeful snowdrops. Edmund sighed mournfully as he remembered his beloved but mischievous friend Peter: until last week, the Almoner (community worker). Though Peter had faithfully delivered parcels to the poor, it was also rumoured he supplied contraband to the Black Market! He was now sadly presumed S.B.F. – Savoured By Feline – (any guardian who hadn't returned from outside within twenty-four hours stood little chance of survival).

Next sat Max the mega-mouse (or rat to everyone else). He'd been found in the precinct one night during the floods, exhausted: his back covered in nasty gashes and his fur matted with human unmentionables from the sewer. Peter had smelt him before he had seen him! He and Ben and Sam had hauled him in – to let him die in peace. But Nathanael not only treated his wounds, but spent weeks shampooing his fur, until at least he was presentable. He should never have been allowed to join the community. He was still unkempt, rather loud and rather large. But again, Brian had persuaded them to accept him, on the condition he didn't sing (his gruff-pitched voice was far too low for their chants). He had been overjoyed however, when Alison had welcomed him into her music club to replace her bass guitar, (which had become awkward to play when she was conducting). Max had since blended well with his neighbour Hikaru, (a Japanese drummer from Tokyo) and Bob (a renowned reggae guitarist from Jamaica) whose stalls followed on.

Next to Bob sat one of the more experienced Guardians, Jan. She, with Lesley (who was the Head of Security and Sub-Prior) were trusted confidants of Marcus the Prior. However, though she was always involved in any top-level discussions, no one was actually sure what Jan did!

As Edmund mused on this quandary, he shook himself awake. Stall III, Paul (the gardener) was there, staring at the ceiling. Stall V, Nathanael (the often truant Infirmary doctor) was there, scribbling in a notebook: but stall VII, the experienced Jan, was definitely NOT there.

'Harry, Harry,' Edmund whispered, 'look!'

'Shhh,' he replied, 'I'm listening to the reading.'

'No, LOOK!' signalled Edmund, and then Harold saw it too. The always reliable Jan was missing.

'We must tell Marcus; we must tell Marcus,' whispered Edmund, 'something's wrong, very wrong. We need to find her immediately!'

Edmund slid down his stall, bowed reverently to the cross on the high table, and hurried off through the organ arch. Finding one of the circular brass lifts, he stamped three times with his foot and began to descend to their quarters.

He went to Jan's room first, just past the lobby on the subterranean quadrangle (or cloister as the human canons called theirs). Edmund knocked gently. 'Sister Jan? Sister Jan?' He tapped again, then slowly pushed on the door and popped his head around. He waggled his whiskers and sniffed, peering into the darkness. 'Jan? Jan? You, ok?'

He felt for the cord and switched on the light. Her bed was neatly made, with a cuddly toy of *Danger Mouse* tucked into her *007* duvet. Her pink fluffy slippers were placed precisely at right angles to her mattress. Her desk was clear, apart from a reading lamp, a writing pad, and three photograph frames (presumably her family?) *No sign of any struggle* he thought. After a glance around the room, he switched off the light and shut the door.

He dashed further along the corridor passing the goldfish bowl of their gym; (the dynamo cycles and hamster wheel – used to supplement power from the Exchange – were silent) – *Not that Jan had a habit of visiting them anyway,* he chuckled. He came to their Dining Hall, which, like all their facilities, mirrored the canons' buildings above. He could see by the green emergency lighting that their tables were deserted and the chairs around them all tilted and empty.

There was no hint of her in the adjoining kitchen either, just the grumble of the dishwasher and the lingering aroma of Gustav's Cheese Pie. (Though Gustav was very popular and an amazing cook – originally from a Temple in France – his attempt at porridge turned out to be more like superglue than superfood.)

Dutifully he checked the fromagerie at the back. The stainless-steel vats and tops were mirror-clean, and he smiled at his spoon-shaped reflection. When he entered the Cheese Grotto, the chilled air slapped his skin, sending waves of shivers down his spine. Each creation resembled a large pork pie and was carefully labelled on a shelf in alphabetical order, like a well-organised library.

Edmund doubled back and checked the chapter house: a rather plain heptagonal room, with chairs around the walls. (This was where the guardians gathered to discuss and make their decisions.) Everything was in darkness.

'Jan, Jan,' he called, but there was no sign of her anywhere. He accepted there was no reason for her to be there anyway. 'Oh Jan!' Edmund sighed and scampered back along the cloister towards the lifts.

The only other building where she could possibly be, was the Dean's Keep – but this was only accessible from the grounds, and he knew it wasn't safe to go 'up-top' alone.

Edmund returned to the cathedral just as prayers were ending, shrugging his shoulders at Harold as he skidded into his stall. Marcus fixed him with his gaze above his pince-nez spectacles and calmly but authoritatively pointed at Edmund, turned his wrist upwards and then bent his finger up slowly, twice. Edmund went rigid, bowed, then purposefully made his way over to the Prior's stall. Marcus leant towards him, lowering his head to hear what Edmund had to say. Edmund spoke energetically, waving his arms as he did so and pausing for breath every few words.

'You say there's no sign of Jan?' clarified Marcus.

'Not a whisker,' replied Edmund, then he looked embarrassed as he realised what he'd said.

Marcus formed a sort of triangle with the tips of his fingers and placed them to his mouth (as he always did when he was concentrating), and then stared up at the starlight ceiling as if listening for advice. A few moments later he looked down at Edmund.

'Thank you, Edmund, we can only hope she has not gone the way of our dearly departed Peter.'

Marcus stood and held up his arm.

One by one, all fell silent.

Marcus cleared his throat: 'It has come to my attention,' he announced, 'that Guardian Jan appears to have rendered herself… mislaid.'

There was a loud murmur of anxiety, and Guardian Petunia fainted, adeptly caught again by Robinson. The guardians were genuinely worried, they were only just beginning to get over the loss of Peter – and now another had vanished without a trace?

'I'm sure there's nothing to worry about,' calmed the Prior, making the sign of the cross out of respect for their erstwhile colleague, or out of repentance for his unproven optimism. 'But we must suspect a security breach and respond accordingly. No-one is to be out alone.' He turned to Lesley, 'Would you organise search parties please, no less than three in a group?'

'Certainly Marcus,' the Sub-Prior replied.

Marcus continued, 'First we must check the perimeters. Then we must do a thorough search of our quarters. I'd like her to be found before we retire. Obviously, no-one is to go *up-top*, the felines will be abroad. We will re-assemble in the safety of the chapter house in…' he pulled out his pocket-watch, 'thirty minutes.'

All nodded. Guardian Lesley took her position on the opposite step and began sending teams out.

CHAPTER 3 — DANGER AND DISASTER

Outside, Robbie began to feel cold. A sprinkling of moss and buds suddenly dusted his hair. He looked up. Two lifeless emerald eyes were moving towards him.

Robbie hated cats, even feared them. His scream as a young boy, when one had ripped into his cheek with razor talons, had never left him – nor had the scars. His breathing quickened as he sought his escape, but he was too high up to jump. More sweat seeped onto his brow as the large cat, with curious forward-folded ears, more like an owl than a feline, stalked nearer, hissing and preparing to pounce.

He had no option but to attack. *Whomp*. He brandished the brass telescope with surprising accuracy, forcing the beast to leap to avoid it, and flop down to the ground with a snarl. Robbie glanced down from side to side, but had it really moved on? Or was it skulking in ambush? He waited a minute, then deftly, lowered himself to the branch below and jumped, landing on all fours on the grass below.

No sooner had he stood and brushed the soil from his hands than the beast reappeared, leapt through the air and seized his boot, swiping at his ankle.

'*Ow*!' Robbie was furious as well as hurt. He kicked it off and raised his telescope in menace. 'I'll get you this time,' he spat. But it turned, and disappeared, vaulting a low garden wall.

Cautiously, Robbie checked behind him then backed himself to the entrance, holding his scope high, ready to swing. *Had it really gone?* he questioned. When his back hit the gates, he continued scouring the darkness, wondering if he dare turn around to climb them. His dad's old saying, *it's now or never* (a song by Elvis?) came to mind: so swiftly he turned and scuttled up the ironwork, dreading talons tearing into his calf.

He reached the top, *Phew*! But immediately checked back – convinced he wasn't quite safe yet. Everything was still, so he hooked his leg over and dropped to the other side of the gate.

The city was silent but well lit. He made his way towards the castle, passing the aromatic Coffee House and Tollie, the museum, on one side, and the amazing bookshop (a labyrinth of a Georgian Townhouse) on the other. As usual, the dual carriageway was completely still (it reminded him of the annual firework display when the roads were always closed off). The castle keep kept watch suspiciously, as it had done for nine hundred years, silhouetted against the glistening-coal sky. The gatehouse, however, was bathed in yellow light like a great arch window. Robbie turned towards the river, tracing the wall of the fortifications.

Negotiating the steps of the flood defences, he crossed the empty car park and entered the park. This was his second-most favourite place to stargaze.

Though he knew he had to hurry home before his dad woke up, he couldn't resist a quick search of the skies. It was a clear night and there was a full moon, so he excitedly extracted his scope from his jacket to explore some of its craters. It wasn't the most powerful scope, you could see far more with the modern ones, but he liked its brass coating and the way you could extend its three sections like a sea-captain. It had also cost him nothing – Mr. Armstrong, his singing teacher, had given it to him the day after his mam had left.

Although he was only six, Robbie could remember that day as if it were only yesterday. It was hometime, everyone was being picked up; the classroom was full of noise and chatter, as mams and dads and grannies reminded their kids to put their coats on or bring their lunch boxes. His best friend Catherine waved 'bye to him as her mam checked she had her reading book and led her away. It all seemed normal, until all the grown-ups and children funnelled out of the door and then out the gates – and Robbie was left alone.

His teacher, Miss Hannah, told him not to worry, that she was sure his mam was just running late. 'Go and sit in the Story Corner,' she suggested. 'Pick any book you like.'

He ran his fingers along the different shelves as if choosing one; but though his eyes were aware of the engaging colours and titles – his mind, his heart, each second before him just seemed frozen, dead, numb, empty. *Where was she?* He didn't know what to do, he wasn't sure where he was; he just knew he didn't want to be there. He could hear Miss Hannah on the phone, talking, but couldn't tell any of the words. He closed his eyes trying to sleep, but all he could see was darkness.

Then something weird happened. Within the abyss of his fear, tiny lights appeared, no, stars! And when he opened his eyes again, there, directly in front of him, was a book called *The Night Sky*. He needed both hands to drag it off the shelf, but when he opened it, he saw this gadgee holding a bow and arrow – well, the outline of one – created by… stars. In his heart, if not his body, he fell into that page and was able to lose himself, lose the agony flowing through him, just for a moment.

He then heard his dad's voice saying sorry and asking if he was all right. And he'd just said, 'Yes': not because he was, but because he had no words for the darkness within him.

Stars had always brought him solace since. Something about there never being total darkness ever, our universe being crammed with stars, with light – most we weren't even able to see. Even a black hole, a dead star, he'd read recently, could sometimes *sick up* a new one – a star it had sucked in centuries before.

He was grateful to his dad, too. At first Geoffrey had gone out with him stargazing, but had soon lost interest, and instead restricted Robbie to their back garden. Eventually, he'd allowed him to go further afield. But on his eleventh birthday, Robbie had finally persuaded his dad to let him stay out till ten o'clock, as long as he had his phone on him – and Geoffrey could track him. (Though Robbie rarely came home on time – or after checking in, would often sneak out again!)

Robbie swallowed hard as he relived that day in the classroom again. His eyes were smarting and began to blur the moon. *Some mam!* he concluded. Wiping the tears with his sleeve, he closed his telescope, he fled towards the river, climbed the steps to the bridge and ambled across the deserted road – his thoughts returning to what he had seen in the cathedral.

He began to doubt himself. *Had he fallen asleep and dreamt it all? Had he slipped and hit his head?*

It was then he felt something trickle onto the top of his boot. He stopped and dabbed it with his fingers – they came back red. *That horrible cat* he deduced, wiping the blood onto his camouflage trousers. Hopefully he didn't need to go to A and E as before; but more importantly, *how was he going to explain such a deep scratch to his dad? Would he twig he'd been out late again?*

He picked up speed, taking the path along the Scaur, which overlooked the sinister black river below. He reached the bottom of his road and glanced up the hill.

The narrow street was a dead end, with cars parked on the left, the river's side, rather than outside the houses on the right. The pavements were helpfully dark, apart from the occasional circle illuminated by a streetlamp. He set off, walking quickly.

As he neared his house, he realised Mr. Armstrong, who lived a few doors down, was still up. Bernard was sitting in a large armchair, pipe in mouth, happily conducting an orchestra in his oversized headphones. His garden path was lit with red solar lamps – because he'd read somewhere that they deterred snails! He'd kindly given some to Robbie's dad too: which was doubly embarrassing because THEY had no hedge, and everyone could see their path lit up like a toy runway!

Robbie crouched, exhausted, knowing he couldn't risk being seen. He got down on his hands and knees to use the hedge for cover. On reaching the ginnel next to his house, he turned off the street and slipped around the back.

A low growl awaited him: *Tutha* the neighbour's pointer rushed towards him.

'It's ok girl,' he comforted, 'it's only me.'

Fortunately, she started wagging her tail and he bent down and gently stroked her nose through the fencing.

He loved Tutha. He felt he could talk to her, and she always seemed to understand. On more than one occasion, he had opened his heart and she had snuggled up to him and licked away his tears.

He'd told Catherine, the most beautiful girl in the world – well, he corrected himself, sighing, a girl who lived at the top of the street – he'd told her once about Tutha, and to his surprise, she hadn't laughed but said it was really important to share your feelings, tell someone how you felt – someone you could trust. She then DID smile, suggesting that a PERSON who could listen and respond, might be a bit more useful than a dog!?

Robbie had thought of Mr. Hyland, his new form tutor, who always had time for him and always seemed to know when he was feeling down. Or there was Pete, the community coach from Corliol United, who'd once told them that he'd grown up without a dad – but still made it as a professional, mostly due to the support of his youth coach.

He'd never forgotten Pete's talk one Saturday, when they were all in tears after losing six nil: 'You've got to let others in,' he'd pushed, 'otherwise you just listen to your own inner voice – and that always puts you down.'

Tutha's cold, wet nose brought him round.

'Good girl,' Robbie praised. 'Quiet girl – Bed!'

She returned to her kennel in disappointment. *Maybe it was the same for dogs?* He thought. *She never barked if he made the time to speak to her.*

Slowly Robbie straightened up and inched his eyes above the fencing. *No movement inside, brill! Dad's still asleep.*

Then, wedging his telescope inside his camouflage jacket, he scrambled over, strode up the path and pulled out the key (hung on a string around his neck).

In seconds, he was through the kitchen door and locking it behind him. He listened – nothing but the buzz of the fridge. *Great.* He crept up the stairs (avoiding number three and seven which always creaked).

His dad, who had grounded him for a whole week the last time he had caught him out so late, was mercifully snoring heavily. Robbie felt his way along the landing to his bedroom and quietly squeezed the door shut behind him.

Phew! He listened once more, then sighed and began slipping off his jacket. But when he reached for his phone in his inside pocket, something furry touched his finger, then it squeaked!

'What the...,' he stuttered, slinging it off in panic. He jumped on the bed and reached for his bedside lamp.

Then he saw it, crawling out of his sleeve. There, in his house – no, in his very bedroom – was... a mouse, and not just any mouse! A mouse with a long black coat buttoned down the centre, a mouse with neat blonde hair, and to his horror, a sort of human face with earrings and lipstick! *One of THOSE mice!* Even worse, instead of scurrying away, she was standing defiantly – with hands on hips – looking rather cross.

'And who might you be?' announced the mouse commandingly, sniffing around the room.

'I'm... I'm Robbie,' he stammered, then came to his senses. 'Never mind me! Who the heck are you?' he exploded.

‘Shhh,’ the figure continued, ‘keep your voice down, do you want the whole street to know I’m here?’

And with that she scrambled across the parquet floor up his desk-leg to the windowsill and began pacing up and down, checking the back street. She turned to face him.

‘Do you think we were followed?’

‘Followed? It’s one in the morning! There’s no one about!’

‘It’s not YOUR lot I’m worried about,’ she explained, ‘have you seen any cats?’

Robbie knew mice didn’t like cats, but she seemed unnaturally frightened.

‘Not many around here,’ he assured her, ‘Tutha sees to that.’

‘Tutha?’

‘Next door’s dog – it’s a pointer.’

The mouse was about to relax but then they both heard the drone of a car approaching. They looked at each other nervously.

‘I’ll go and have a look,’ whispered Robbie.

‘You’ll do nothing of the sort,’ the mouse fired back, then, ‘Shhh.’

They both froze; and sure enough, they heard an engine running, a blast of music, then a door slam, and the car drive off.

‘Now you can go and check,’ the mouse authorised.

Robbie tiptoed out onto the landing.

A second later he was back. ‘No-one there,’ he assured, ‘must have been a taxi.’

‘Taxi?’

‘Probably Mrs Truelove, she works shifts at the hospital and lives at the top. They always drop her off at the bottom, so they don’t have to reverse all the way back.’

‘Hmm,’ came the reply. ‘Disaster, disaster, I told them this would never work!’

‘Told who?’

‘Never you mind,’ she scolded, then added, ‘typical *Shallownessian*, too nosy for their own good. Let’s just say you’re not the person I was supposed to meet.’

‘Shallow what?’ Robbie enquired.

‘*Shallownessian,*’ she explained, ‘it’s what we call your kind, because you’re so shallow.’

Robbie grimaced, mystified. *Shallow? Shallow? He was much bigger than them!*

‘The way you live,’ she continued, exasperated; then added with a giggle, ‘My dear boy, what else would you call a people who spent all their time *getting* and *spending*, rather than *giving* and *caring*? On *doing* and *producing,* rather than *appreciating* and just *being*?’

Then her eye caught Robbie’s *Small Soldiers* duvet cover, and the camouflage netting pinned to his wall.

‘Fancy ourselves in the S.A.S. do we?’

Robbie blushed a little. ‘I used to, when I was younger.’

He shuffled sideways, trying to hide his collection of Lego tanks!

‘Hmmm,’ the mouse sighed, unconvinced; but to Robbie’s relief, changed the subject. ‘And this?’ she asked, nudging a small trophy on the windowsill, ‘Runner-up? What? Shooting?’

‘Not quite,’ Robbie coughed, ‘singing.’

A proud smile spread across his face as he relived the greatest night of his life: the final of C.G.T. (Corliol’s

Got Talent). Three thousand faces looking up at him, burning lights and T.V. cameras looking down; and most of all: Catherine, secretly giving him a *thumbs up* in the front row, flanked by her parents. (Oh, and his dad and Mr. Armstrong, a few seats along.)

'And now our final contestant,' the host announced, 'the City's own singing sensation… Robbie Harraby!'

The backing track began, he took a deep breath, and heard his voice melting into the melody. He tried not to think of the end, because Mr. Armstrong had insisted he not only sung Mariah Carey's version of *A Whole New World*, (with what his dad called squeaky additions); but, to show off his voice, he was to go up several octaves on the last note (his specialty).The music built; the audience leaned forwards, Robbie filled his lungs, squeezed his vocal chords and let it go. *Yes! YES!* his inner voice erupted, as his outer voice rocketed triumphantly. The hall broke out in applause. Kids and teenagers began to stand, but as he turned to the judges, they were simply talking among themselves! His dad sat puzzled too (at his age, like all the adults, he could not hear such a high note – neither could the judges) – and THAT was Robbie's downfall.

Realising the mistake, Mr. Armstrong slumped forward, shaking his head in disappointment and coughing uncontrollably.

But Robbie just felt bathed in warmth, ten feet tall; because the one person that mattered, was on her feet, staring him straight in the eyes and beaming adoringly – the wonderful Catherine.

Jan yawned.

Robbie came around.

'Hello?' Jan sang sarcastically.

'Oh, er, sorry,' Robbie eventually replied.

'A great evening then?'

Robbie grinned again, but then looked a little fazed – had he said coming second had been 'great'? Before he had a chance to press her, Jan continued her interrogation.

'So, what were you doing outside the Temple tonight?'

'Temple?' questioned Robbie.

'Cathedral then.'

'Well,' answered Robbie proudly, 'I'm an astronomer and I go out at night to watch the stars.'

'Oh dear, oh dear,' replied the mouse, 'first a singer, now one of THEM. This IS a disaster.'

'Anyway,' pushed Robbie, 'how come you have a face and can speak, and how come you are dressed like that?'

'My dear boy,' sighed the rodent, closing her eyes, 'my name is Jan, Guardian Jan to you – and I'm an agent of Corliol – that's all you need to know.'

Robbie wasn't going to stop there. '*Corliol*, what the heck is *Corliol*?'

Jan shook her head in disbelief. 'Don't they teach you anything at school?'

Robbie just looked blank.

'Corliol is where the Guardians live.'

'What guardians?'

'The Guardians of the Temple.'

'What Temple?'

'I've already told you, that great pink edifice you were prowling around tonight, you numpty,' came the reply.

'The cathedral's a Temple?'

'Obviously,' sighed Jan, 'so at night…'

'What?'

Jan threw her arms up in despair. 'Look, there's no time for this now, we have to find my Shallownessian contact.'

'We?' cautioned Robbie.

'Well, you don't expect me to wander the streets alone do you, with so many feline monsters about?'

Monsters? Thought Robbie, but then he remembered how unusually large and vicious that cat had been to him and understood what damage it could do to her.

'They're not just ordinary cats,' Jan continued, 'and they'll kill to get into your…,' Jan paused, 'cathedral.'

Robbie thought it was all *over the top*. He didn't like cats but didn't think one would ever try to kill him! And what could they possibly want from the cathedral? Robbie tried not to laugh.

'Believe me,' Jan pleaded, 'you have no idea.'

I can't tell him about the ceiling stars and their true worth, she decided. *He's just a boy, and it's probably best to keep him out of sight of the cats. Nor can I tell him he wouldn't be the first Shallownessian to die at their talons – he'd have nightmares for weeks! If he can just get me back to the Temple that will be enough.*

'Look, I need to get back there right away. It would be much safer if you took me?'

'Sorry,' Robbie apologised, 'I can't go out again, not now. There's no telling when dad might wake up and notice I'm not here. He grounded me for a whole week last time!'

Jan sighed. 'Right, take me to your father.'

'Why? What are you going to do?'

'Don't worry, I won't harm him; just make him sleep a little more deeply. Well, come on, pick me up.'

Robbie reluctantly held out his hand towards the windowsill and Jan scampered onto his arm then up to his shoulder. He could feel her sharp claws pattering on his skin and a shiver went down his spine: *I hope she hasn't got fleas* he thought; and almost in response Jan turned and looked him straight in the eyes. Robbie paused, then feigned: 'What?'

She just shook her head slowly then turned to face forward again. Cautiously, Robbie tiptoed into his dad's bedroom, avoiding a discarded mug and plate on the floor. Geoffrey was snoring loudly.

'He's not always this bad, he's got a cold,' whispered Robbie.

In Robbie's eyes, his dad was a good but *funny* bloke. He had always been there for Robbie, especially when his mam had left. But the house was much less tidy, even a bit of a tip – though Robbie liked the way he could leave his Lego out and his bed unmade. They didn't talk much (Geoffrey wasn't good at conversation), but Robbie knew if he ever needed to, Geoffrey would always sit and listen – even if he had nothing to say in return! It was what he missed most about his mam – she was really good at chatting; but there again, for all Geoffrey's faults, *HE* was the one that had stayed, *HE* was the one that must really love him.

Jan leapt onto the bottom of the bed, wincing at each elongated snore. Robbie stepped closer. 'SShh,' Jan chided, then suddenly CRUNCH! Robbie had stepped on an empty beer can. Geoffrey's eyes shot open.

I've had it now shook Robbie. But as his dad turned towards them, Jan was already in position, at his ear, offering a beguiling chant.

'Our hearts are restless till they rest in you, you are much nearer than we are to you. Oh, come within us, let your love abide, now let your presence draw us to your side.'

Geoffrey, his eyes still focused on Jan, seemed to be completely oblivious of what he was seeing. Jan gently stroked his eyelids shut, and he sank back into his pillow with a relaxed smile across his face. His head swayed gently to the chant, and he dozed off sighing, rather than snoring.

It's so relaxing, agreed Robbie as HIS eyelids began to close too, until Jan, noticing, climbed up onto his neck.

'Ow!' he jumped, as her claws spiked his skin.

'NOW can we go?' she begged.

Robbie gazed affectionately at his dad. Yes, he had untidy eyebrows and hair hanging out of his nostrils and ears, but he wasn't bad looking. Seeing him sleeping, smiling, with a day or so's stubble outlining his cheeks, lips and chin (like the shadow of a beard) almost made him cute. He didn't blame his dad for telling him off. Robbie accepted that any parent would ban their child from sneaking out at night alone. He knew it was dangerous too. But he had his phone and was very careful – and he just loved the stars!'

Jan waved her arms to get his attention.

Robbie eventually snapped out of it and tried to act interested. 'That's amazing!' he mumbled. 'How long will he sleep for?'

Jan placed her finger to her lips and looking back at him, whispered: 'Hard to tell. But unless there's a massive disturbance, he should sleep for at least six hours.'

'But won't he remember you?'

'He'll think it was all a *lovely* dream.' She giggled, 'The chants are great, aren't they?'

Robbie couldn't help but rub his hands in glee – he could go out again!

'I'll go and check the street; you get your coat,' commanded Jan, running down ahead of him.

Robbie then remembered his ankle. He went to the bathroom, found an antiseptic wipe and gently dabbed his wounds. One was quite deep and very red. He searched for a plaster, but they were all too small. Fortunately, he found an adhesive sterile dressing and smoothed it on with a wince. Returning to his bedroom, he grabbed his jacket and commando phone and hurried back to the landing where Jan was waiting. Soon she was on his shoulder, and he was creeping down the stairs.

In less than a minute, they were unbolting the back gate. Robbie checked there was no-one about, called 'Bed!' to an approaching Tutha, then turned and set off down the street.

As Robbie came to Mr. Armstrong's, he dropped onto his hands and knees. He scoured the path beneath him as best as he could, not wanting to place his palm in anything horrible. (Not all dog-owners were responsible.) He froze as a beetle scurried across his hand. But as he placed his other hand beyond his gaze, his worst fears came true. He touched something soft, well, hard -and-soft, and uncomfortably warm. Slowly he lifted his eyes. 'Oh,' he mumbled.

In the middle of the night, on his own street, he found his hand on top of a woman's shoe. This wouldn't have been too bad if the shoe hadn't been occupied and accompanied by another. *Aaah* he sighed to himself in disappointment, as he traced the shoe to a stockinged ankle, then shin, then coat, then the face of Mrs Truelove looking down at him in disbelief. Robbie forced a smile.

'Um, er, Catherine all right is she Mrs Truelove?'

There was an awkward pause.

'Yes Robbie, thank you,' she replied, then added sarcastically, 'she's an unusual girl though, at this time of night she tends to be in bed!'

Robbie grimaced, his eyes slowly looking one way then the other, lost as to what to say. Then, it came to him: 'You haven't seen a pound coin anywhere, have you? I think I lost one this afternoon?'

Mrs Truelove didn't reply, just slowly shook her head.

'Have a good night then,' Robbie added, dreading what she'd say to Catherine.

'Perhaps if you took your hand off my shoe I could?' she replied.

Robbie immediately let go; 'Yes, yes, sorry Mrs Truelove.' And with that she stepped around him, but oddly, as he watched, she seemed less than keen to hurry up the hill, more like dawdling than anything, and kept turning back, as if checking he'd gone.

'So, Catherine lives up the road?' concluded Jan. Then, turning to face him, she batted her eyelids and added, melodramatically, 'How *lovely.*'

Robbie frowned, bewildered. *How does she know I like Catherine?*

'Not to worry,' said Jan, 'come on, *chop-chop*!'

Once they had passed Mr. Armstrong's, Robbie stood up and sprinted down the hill, forgetting poor Jan was in his top pocket holding on for dear life.

CHAPTER 4 — THE BETRAYAL

No more than a couple of miles away, in the cellar of the local biscuit factory, cats were gathered around a large oak table. Their leader Satan, a black Siberian, had just finished his lecture on how to detect, charm, then kill mice. He then moved on to his grand plan.

'It's only a matter of time before we get a star,' he assured them. 'Those foolish mice have no idea we have all we need,' – he nodded towards his office – 'thanks to our *friend*.'

They all began to smile. Luci, a golden Persian with sultry eyes and a diamond necklace (his second in command), was the only one to respond.

'He has outlived his usefulness, no?'

'Not quite, my *printsessa*,' the silken black Siberian replied, 'let's keep him till tonight when we will have our star. THEN you can have him.'

Luci licked her lips.

Satan spread a large pencil drawing of the cathedral grounds on the table. 'Come comrades, gather round!'

'We goin' tonight *den*, Boss?' asked M.C., an enormous Maine Cat from Brooklyn.

'Obviously,' barked Hunter, adding a naughty word in Afrikaans.

Hunter was the most dangerous of them all, the epitome of a leopard – except slightly smaller, as if he'd been shrunk in the wash. Even Satan was careful around him – recognising a rival for the pride's leadership elections later that year. Satan had already seen off his previous challenger, Alex, who had disagreed with the whole direction Satan was taking them. After months of arguing, Alex had simply disappeared, though all knew his last sighting had been alongside the river, late at night, with Satan and Luci.

Next in seniority came Yak and Uza, two overgrown Siamese (Luci's Ninja bodyguards,) complete with face-masks – obedient, attentive, but highly trained assassins. The rest varied in size and ability – some more dangerous than others.

'Once inside,' announced Satan, 'There is no way they can hold us off.'

'But what about the sentinels?' questioned Ho Lee, leader of the Dragon Li Triad – five extremely savage but agile cats from China.

'The gargoyles? They won't activate till later and our Indian friends Sun, Dar and Singh, will have it all in hand.'

The small cats each placed their paws together, bowed their turbaned heads, and in chorus replied *'Na-ma-ste'*.

Satan then turned to the rest of his ginger toms, his favourite cat burglars. 'I have a little task for you. Luci will fully brief you, but you need to assist your comrades in bringing in as much porridge as you can.'

They looked at each other: *Porridge?*

'Raid every shop, every home. I don't care where you get it from, just get it to me. Do you understand?'

The ginger toms nodded in assent.

'And I want a glass bowl with a screw-top lid, and a small mirror.'

'Yes, master,' they replied.

Luci called them over and gave them their instructions. Apparently, she'd seen some glass sweet bowls in a bank in the city centre. They would be perfect, once they'd carefully removed the sweets, of course! (The felines hated sticky bon bons – they always got matted in their fur.)

Suddenly, the door flew open, and a large cat with forward-folded ears bounded down the steps – it was one of the Scottish-fold twins – Burke and Hare – deceptively cute-looking, but with piercing claws.

'Sorry master,' it bowed, 'but I think a Guardian has just escaped with a human boy.'

'Did you not stop them?' Satan snarled.

'He was too quick, and I was alone, Hare was patrolling the other side of the Temple.'

'You couldn't even stop a boy?'

'Master, he had a weapon!'

Satan struck the table with his fist, in anger. 'Which way did they go?'

'Not sure. They might still be there. Hare is looking for them.'

Satan turned to his struggling pride and pointed to those nearest the lair.

'Right, you brainless serfs, come with me – the rest of you watch our little friend.'

Immediately twenty or so cats followed him out the door, with Luci bringing up the rear.

#

In the abandoned office, in a dark corner, in a metal cage, a tiny figure in a chubby black coat was in turmoil, tears gushing down its cheeks. It was Peter.

'What have I done?' he cried, 'I'm so sorry, so sorry.'

He was in the vicious circle of reliving his cowardice and stupidity over and over again.

It had started well: the felines had been lovely. He could still feel the luxurious soft cushions on which they had originally placed him. He had suspected nothing. He was sure he could work out a deal for the *Dandelion and Burdock* shipment which could bring mutual benefit to both of them.

'Have another custard cream,' Satan had smiled.

'I don't mind if I do,' Peter heard himself replying. He could just hear the faint whirr of the Shallownessian machinery on the floor above and was high on the distinct scent of ginger drifting through the air vents.

'See,' Satan had continued, 'it's much better to be friends, isn't it? And what difference will one little solar system, one little, inkle, star make among so many?'

Peter had closed his eyes in bliss as he nibbled into the cream.

'And isn't it good to share?'

'Ok.' Peter had said. 'But only one star.'

'Of course,' replied Satan, pursing his lips sympathetically, 'Now, how do we get one?'

'Well, you'd have to get in first,' Peter had chuckled.

'You leave that to me,' Satan had replied.

'Don't forget the Scoobies!' warned Peter.

'The Scoobies?'

'The gargoyles,' Peter explained, sighing as if to say *obviously*. 'You won't get in if you wake THEM!'

'I thought they wouldn't activate till one o'clock when the portals open? And we'll already be in by then.'

Peter chuckled, 'Yes but you'll never get out, will you?'

Satan looked troubled. He hadn't planned on the Scoobies being there as they left.

'And there's no way to stop them?'

'No.' Then Peter thought for a moment, 'Unless…'

'Unless what?'

'Unless, before they activate, you could somehow paralyse them?'

Satan huffed, rather defeated. *How on earth would they do that? They were at least several metres up the cathedral tower.*

Suddenly Peter sat up. 'Porridge!' he chirped.

'What?'

'Gustav's porridge! He makes it with cream and adds salt rather than sugar, and it dries as hard as concrete. We spilt some on one of the statues once and it couldn't move for hours until we'd washed it all off. His porridge will paralyse anything.'

Satan signalled to Luci, who efficiently detailed it in her notebook. Satan turned back to Peter.

'So. Once inside, how do we trap a star?'

'Well,' said Peter, happily munching away. 'I've never done it myself... but they say you need a mirror, a glass bowl, and a lid.'

Luci wrote it down meticulously. Peter had gazed at her beautiful cheeks and large brown eyes, *for a feline she wasn't half...* Suddenly he was brought down to earth as Satan clicked his fingers in front of him and moved Peter's snout back to look him in the eyes.

'And?'

'And,' Peter munched, 'you lay the mirror at the bottom of the bowl.'

'And?'

'And you flash at one or two of the planets as they fly past.'

'And?' Satan leant forward.

'And at least one of the planets is bound to enter the bowl to investigate. They're very inquisitive, you know planets… I remember when one of them…'

'Yes, yes, then what?'

'Well,' Peter continued, wiping crumbs off his whiskers, 'when it sees its reflection in the mirror, it will think it has a twin!'

'Hmmm?'

'Before long, it will have called another of its sister planets to have a look; and in minutes, you'll have the whole star, the whole solar system, wondering at their reflections too.'

Peter burped. 'That's when you do it.'

'Do what?'

'Screw the lid on silly.'

'And that's it? They can't get out?'

'Nope, you've got them for good. They'll probably re-absorb themselves into a star, but they'll all be in there.'

Before Peter had finished his last mouthful Satan had snatched the biscuit out of his mouth and two of his henchtoms, M.C. and Hunter, had dragged Peter back-wards into a waiting cage, which they padlocked securely.

Peter sobbed again as he remembered Satan licking his paws slowly and deliberately in satisfaction. Then how he had stared at his talons, and without turning his head, simply said to Luci, 'Tonight I will have my star.'

#

As Prior Marcus entered the chapter house, everyone (apart from Harold who was deep in thought in his chairicopter) stood respectfully, and the chatter faded immediately. He looked troubled as he moved to the Prior's seat, bearing the Temple's Coat of Arms (a black cross on a white shield). He hesitated for a while then looked round his flock who were standing attentively in their customary circle.

Marcus noticeably paused at the two empty spaces where Peter and Jan should have been. He cleared his throat: 'It is clear that our dear sister Jan is not,' he paused, 'with us.'

There was a gasp from the assembly, and Petunia fell back onto her chair.

The Prior continued, 'If she is abroad' (which meant 'up top') 'we can only pray that she will make her way back in the next hour or so before the Temple is sealed. Otherwise,' he paused again, as several guardians looked at each other, 'she will have a whole day at the mercy of the felines.'

A sharp intake of breath worked its way around the circle like a Mexican wave.

'Now, is there anything else we need to discuss?'

There was another pause, then a rather plain mouse, distinguishable only by the large wellington boots on his feet, raised his arm.

'Yes, Paul?' Marcus invited.

'It's about my dandelions,' began the Guardian Gardener, in a heavy west country accent. 'They're still dis'pearing at a rate o' knots.'

The image of flowers being removed 'at a rate of knots' for a moment puzzled the Prior. The assembled company broke out into a flurry of whispers. Marcus placed his hands together in resolve.

'Brothers and sisters,' he called, 'I thought we had all agreed that Paul's poly-tunnel of dandelions was for medicinal purposes only and should only be accessed through Guardian Nathanael, our infirmarian.'

(Who was now treating Petunia with smelling salts, well, some fluff from one of Maximus's socks.)

There was general consent and nodding of heads, though a few, including Ben and Nat curiously seemed to be averting their gaze by staring up at the vaulted ceiling; and one, Guardian William, conspicuously stared at his feet or foot, with his remaining eye.

'Do I detect,' continued the Prior, 'that you wish to re-open our discussion about these plants? Or are some of our number purposely deciding to reject our chapter's will?'

The Chapter House fell deathly silent. Although the Prior was indeed their elected leader, and in the ancient rules of their community, more a chairmouse than a *boss;* and although he always worked hard to ensure the guardians made all their decisions together; he was still the Prior: the first among equals.

'May I also remind you,' he continued, 'that though the consumption of Dandelion and Burdock, in measure, is NOT prohibited, its manufacture or distilling on these premises certainly is!'

There was a lot of coughing and foot-shifting from those gathered.

'Perhaps,' suggested Brian, 'this is a one-off, a moment of forgetfulness, no more than a hiccup?'

'Hiccup?' Lip-read Ben and Sam simultaneously, as Guardian William winked at them (which was a little disconcerting as he usually fell over when he did). They immediately grinned and signed to each other, 'We've certainly had more than ONE hiccup!'

'Very well,' concluded the Prior, 'unless anyone has anything else to add? Can I take it that it won't happen again?'

All nodded. It was then that Bob raised his arm.

'Yes Bob?' Marcus encouraged.

Despite being an accomplished lead guitarist (who'd won international acclaim for his hit, *Mouseway to Heaven*), Bob was a very quiet and gentle person. If it wasn't for his oversized red, green, and yellow crocheted cap (which Alison always described as 'simply exquisite') atop his silky dreadlocks, you would hardly ever notice him. The West Indian opened his arms in a pleading gesture and addressed his peers.

'*Mi luv ya'al* brothers and sisters but *mi bad, mi* bed bad,' Bob whimpered out of tiredness.

Marcus looked to Lesley for help.

'Although he loves us all dearly,' she translated, 'Bob's not sleeping well because his mattress is too uncomfortable.'

'I'm sorry to hear that Bob,' empathised the Prior, again looking at Lesley, 'I'm sure we can obtain a new one for you.'

Lesley nodded. An enormous smile revealing a perfect set of pearl-white teeth blossomed across Bob's face.

'*Tank yuh!*' he added, with a dip of his head.

'Anything else?' Marcus checked.

He was met by a hushed silence.

'Now, back to Jan,' he directed, 'Robinson, please seal the portal at the usual time, we can't take any chances. In the meantime, I suggest we all return to our rooms and pray for a miracle.'

There was a heaviness as the room began to empty but Marcus and Lesley began to talk.

'Do you think I should check the *birds*?' she winked.

'Good idea, we've looked everywhere else. In fact, you check the *birds* and I'll join you there as soon as I can.'

#

Lesley calmly took the lift down to their quarters and headed for the Dining Room, (or *Fratry* as the Shallownessians called theirs). The corridors were quiet, so she crossed the floor to the kitchen, and then to the walk-in cheese store. She checked behind her, listened for a second, and then went to the bottom shelf, slipped between the stacks of Gorgonzola and Lancashire Creamy, and whispered, 'Tolfink.'

The wall slid sideways, revealing a cavernous space. She fumbled for the push button on her right and within seconds, a line of crackling bulbs ignited along the tunnel at about mouse height. The musty breath of nine hundred years of war and decay hit her throat and nostrils. Before her lay the secret Shallownessian passage to the castle. It had long since been abandoned and blocked, but unbeknown to most, the senior guardians had brought it back into use as a safe passage to the Dean's Keep.

Lesley whispered again and the shelving shifted back into place. Hurriedly she crossed the rubble-littered shaft knowing she only had a short time to reach the ladder before the timer on the lights ran out. Sure enough, she had just begun to climb the metal rungs when darkness recaptured its domain.

Suddenly a rush of air swept down the tunnel. *There's someone coming*, she quaked; and lunged upwards into the abyss without thought of what might lie ahead. She reached the top in no time but could sense movement below! She froze, not daring to lift the trap door in fear of the light betraying her. She held the rung with one paw and covering her mouth with the other, tried to smother the resounding wood-sawing *give-away* of her rapid breathing.

'Hey! I tell *ya* they've been here, right?' whispered a husky New York accent, 'Can smell 'em. Yeah?'

Lesley tried not to look down but just had to. And there, in the dim light she could see two large cats, each with mining helmets, sniffing the walls. One was thick set and heavy, and wearing a back-to-front baseball cap (on top of the helmet!), and seemed uncertain on his feet. The other was even larger, but slender, sure-footed like a small panther. Lesley held on for grim death as they peered around the enormous structure, their powerful head-torches lighting up the roof like searchlights: *soon lighting her up?* She closed her eyes but couldn't stop shaking, *just don't move, don't move,* she coaxed herself. The cats were now inspecting the walls.

'They must have an exit route, *capiche*?' the first one concluded.

'But where are they going?' the slender one replied, in a South African accent, 'Do *ye* think they've found our kit-hole at Tollie?'

'Could be bro, I guess. What do we do *already*? Huh?' he continued.

'We must inform the master,' the South African concluded, obviously taking the lead.

'Sure thing,' the American agreed looking around a bit lost. 'Dah, …you remember the route back?'

The second muttered something, turned and led the way. Lesley gasped and watched them winding their way through the rubble until the darkness engulfed them. She then released a wheezing cough in relief. *He will send his angels to guard you in all your ways,* she recalled.

Though no longer in immediate danger, her head firmly told her to turn back. Her heart, however, disagreed. Thoughts of Peter, and then Jan, gave her resolve to go on. She pushed the hatch above her and squeezed through into the vaulted cellar. There was a door on the right and some stairs on the left.

She checked there was no-one about with her whiskers, then scampered towards the window, to see if the emergency pane had been used, but it was firmly bolted and covered in cobwebs. She thought about opening it for Jan – after all, it was too small for a cat, – but she knew this was against all the security protocols (last time a squirrel had slipped in, and it had taken them months to force it out).

In fact, etched across it were the words *Emergency Exit Only – Keep closed at all times* (which she had often thought was a very silly instruction, because how could anyone escape, if you had to keep it closed *at ALL times*?) Nevertheless, she accepted it was meant to be an escape not an entrance and had herself insisted it was to be kept sealed unless attended. Disappointed, she headed for the steps, scrambling up one by one to the Prior's room on the first floor.

There was a cacophony of sound: the birds on the ceiling were in full song or mimicking the *Shallownessians* who'd been there that day. Lesley filled her lungs and then let rip: 'Quiet please!'

It took a few minutes for them to settle down.

'Good evening, ladies, and gents! A favour if I may? You haven't seen Guardian Jan, have you?'

'Guardian who? Guardian who?' repeated a parrot.

'Guardian Jan?' cawed a crow, 'The wild one with the spiky hair?'

'No, no,' said Lesley, 'that's Alison.'

'The one with the heavy make-up and lace handkerchief?' clacked another.

'No, no,' she continued, 'that's Petunia.'

'The one who's always banging on about security?' came a low, hoarse, squawk from the Pelican.

'No,' sighed Lesley gruffly, 'that's me!'

'Oh, sorry,' it rasped, embarrassed.

'JAN,' she emphasised, 'Guardian 007!'

'Sorry mother,' sighed, another parrot, 'no-one's been in tonight, no-one's been in tonight,' and quickly they resumed their conversations.

CHAPTER 5 — INTO BATTLE

Robbie, with Jan on his shoulder, soon reached the cathedral grounds. 'Stop,' she commanded, 'wait here,' and she dropped down onto the tarmac. Robbie dutifully stopped.

But as he stretched out a hand to sit by the litter bin he jumped back in horror. 'Errrgh,' he moaned (it was all sticky and surrounded by a pool of dark liquid). He warily sniffed his hand and his face changed. To his surprise, it didn't smell bad at all, quite sweet really – something like Dandelion and Burdock! He looked around for something to wipe his hand on, but within seconds Jan had returned. 'This way,' she whispered.

For a moment, Robbie faltered. *Was he really at the cathedral gates in the middle of the night? Walking behind a talking mouse, searching for overgrown cats? No-one would believe him at school! Did he believe it himself?*

Jan tugged on the hem of his combat trousers impatiently. 'Now!' she insisted, 'come ON!'

Robbie could see that the main gates were still locked.

Jan sniffed the air. 'Felines.'

'Where?'

'I'm not sure, but I can smell them, and there's definitely more than one.'

'I'm not afraid of cats,' said Robbie proudly (and dishonestly).

'Well bully for you,' replied Jan, 'I wouldn't be either, if I were as big as you!' (Equally untruthfully.)

'I know a good place to climb over,' advised Robbie.

‘Certainly not!’ Jan corrected, and with that she zig-zagged up one side of the gates and delicately leapt onto one of the gold baubles at its centre. Then she began whispering something. Incredibly, the bauble moved down under her weight, and even more bewildering, the one next to it, took its place, and a third took ITS position until they were all slowly turning like a hand-powered Ferris Wheel.

Robbie was astounded as the black heavy gates gently opened. Jan scampered down, and with her weight gone, the baubles began moving back to their original positions. Robbie slipped through, just before the gates sealed themselves again.

‘See any Shallow… Em …humans?’ asked Jan.

‘Wait on,’ replied Robbie, and put on some night-vision goggles from his outer pocket. Jan could see him squinting and looking around distractedly. ‘Got them last year,’ he announced proudly.

‘And do they work?’ Jan sighed, doubtfully.

‘I think so,’ Robbie responded, clearly unable to focus on anything, never mind see into the dark.

‘Perhaps you’d be better with the naked eye for now?’ suggested Jan.

‘No, no,’ insisted Robbie, ‘I think my eyes just need to get used to them.’

‘Very well,’ huffed Jan, shaking her head. ‘You’re sure you can’t see any humans then?’

‘Nope,’ Robbie replied, squinting in entirely the wrong direction.

‘Great Tolfink,’ Jan muttered under her breath, *not only do I have a Shallownessian who has no idea what’s going on, but now he can’t even see!* Jan scoured the shadows, then said slowly and deliberately. 'There's something wrong.'

'I knew it, I knew it!' commented Robbie excitedly, 'Just what I thought.'

Jan lifted her eyes to the skies in defeat. Then had an idea. 'How good are you at doing dog impressions?'

'What?'

'You heard.'

'Well, I can sort of bark.' (He used to play at talking to Tutha.)

'Try it then.'

'What now?'

'No next week, when do you think?'

Robbie took a breath then held it. 'I can't,' he said.

'Why not?'

'Not while you're looking at me, I'm feeling all self-conscious.'

'Oh, for goodness' sake!' sighed Jan, turning her back to him.

After what seemed an eternity Robbie responded: 'Gruff- gruff-gruff!'

'Not bad, again!' ordered Jan, scouring the darkness.

'Gruff, gruff, gruff-gruff!'

Despite the lack of light two green eyes appeared from the bushes.

'There!' whispered Jan, 'See him?' But when she glanced up, Robbie was again looking in completely the wrong direction. 'Bark again,' she commanded.

On the left, from along the wall, another pair of eyes appeared.

'Gotcha!' triumphed Jan. 'Right, only two, we should be able to get to the portal ok,' and before Robbie had a chance to respond, she gave her next order. 'Forward towards the main door.'

Then the unthinkable happened – in the darkness THREE pairs of eyes appeared from the stone arch directly in front of them. Robbie also sensed something to his right, and sure enough three gigantic black cats appeared.

'L… l… look!' he whispered, 'you're right, they're, they're, monsters!'

'It's the shadows off the floodlights,' Jan calmed, trying to hide the fact that they were indeed being surrounded.

'You know I said I wasn't afraid of cats,' whispered Robbie, 'well there does seem to be rather a lot of them, and they do seem to be slightly HUGE!'

'It's genetic,' Jan replied, shooting up his trouser leg and appearing at his shoulder, then warning: 'Half of them are technically illegal to own.'

Robbie's heart sank. *That other cat was bad enough – and these were bigger!*

'Shhh,' frowned Jan.

'I didn't say anythi – ' Robbie replied, puzzled.

Both froze as a feline suddenly sprung from the arch-way and landed not a metre in front of them. Though no longer a silhouette, it revealed itself just as black, and, much, much larger than Robbie had thought. In fact, it was the biggest cat he had ever seen; *the size of a dog, no, a bear, no, a dog,* thought Robbie.

When it opened its mouth and began to speak, Robbie calmly accepted it! *Here we go again, he concluded, – if the mice can speak – why shouldn't the cats?* Though as the beast drew nearer, rather reassuringly it showed no human features.

‘Well now, what have we here?’ the enormous cat purred, in a sultry Russian accent.

Jan recognised him as Satan, the Guardian’s arch-enemy.

‘None of your business,’ she replied defiantly, ‘and we’d be grateful if you moved out of our way.’

‘Who’s the human?’ Satan continued.

‘He’s a very strong boy and he doesn’t like cats,’ Jan threatened (to Robbie’s alarm).

‘No need to be aggressive, my little sparrow,’ whispered the cat.

‘Sparrow ?!’ Jan challenged.

‘Ah, forgive me,’ he replied, ‘back in my Motherland.’

‘Russia?’

‘Ah *nyet*, no. I am from Timsk in Siberia – there it is a term of affection, my little *Hors d’Oeuvres.*’

Sniggering and tittering came from the darkness – there were more of them in the shadows!

Robbie had no idea what *Hors d’Oeuvres* meant, but by Jan’s face, he knew it wasn’t good.

Jan was carefully weighing up their options. Could she at least delay the attack? ‘How about a deal?’ she proffered.

Satan slowly turned his head to one side inquisitively. Then, suddenly burst out laughing, accompanied by the now twenty or so cats surrounding them. Halfway through a laugh, he stopped, and the others immediately fell silent (apart from an enormous Maine Cat wearing a baseball cap, who laughed on and on – until he noticed everyone, including Jan and Robbie, looking at him in despair). Quickly, he changed his laughing into a nervous cough and struck his chest, feigning a choking fit.

‘You KNOW what I want,’ Satan continued.

‘Out of the question,’ Jan replied, ‘the stars are the Maker’s – not yours.’

‘You know I’ll get one sooner or later,’ he sighed.

‘Over my dead body,’ she countered.

Satan didn’t reply, he just flicked out his talons, one by one, and licked his paw as if savouring a tasty treat. Then he made a circling gesture with his wrist and his pride began to close in.

Suddenly, the air exploded with the sound of submachine gun fire!

The cats scattered. Satan, in panic, turned to flee and collided with two of his henchmen.

Jan dived into Robbie’s front pocket (though later, she realised, if a bullet had hit her, the cloth would have made little difference).

Robbie alone held his ground, and reached for his phone: ‘Oh no,’ he screeched, pulling out the still-firing ringtone, ‘it’s my dad!’

‘Where the heck are you?’ shouted a voice, ‘It’s way past ten!’

‘Dad?’ Robbie called, lost for words.

‘Sing! Sing!’ Jan instructed.

Robbie began to sing: ‘I can show you the world…’

‘No, no, OUR song,’ she corrected.

‘I’ve told you before,’ Geoffrey, lectured… But as soon as Robbie began to hum Jan’s high-pitched song, he fell silent. ‘Hmm,’ he yawned, ‘nighty, nighty.’

And the line went dead.

‘Forget him, he’ll be fine!’ recovered Jan, ‘just make for the arch, NOW!’

Without thinking, Robbie hurtled forwards, conscious of more and more pairs of eyes and shadows resurfacing from behind walls and bushes. Jan leapt from his pocket, surfed down his leg and placed two paws on the stonework. 'Do this,' she screamed, 'NOW! You're just going to have to come with me.'

With so many eyes rushing towards him, Robbie didn't hesitate and placed his hands just like hers. Jan muttered something, and within seconds, Robbie felt himself falling forwards into darkness.

#

The cats flooded the arch, feeling for some secret button or opening, but in vain. 'Search the grounds!' ordered Satan. His pride leapt onto car bonnets and roofs, clawed up trees, forced open the black bins, but found nothing. 'Check the main entrance!' ordered Satan as a last resort.

But as they threw themselves against the heavy wooden doors, they foolishly awoke the sentinels above them, and a terrifying howl overwhelmed the grounds, soon echoed by others. Odd lights came on in some of the canons' houses, and eventually, all the lights came on in the Verger's lodge.

'Retreat! Retreat!' screamed Satan, 'it's the Scoobies!'

The dog-like gargoyles swooped down from the tower like miniature dragons, baring enormous teeth and salivating profusely. Ho Lee, the leader of the Dragon Li was bitten, and many were swiped by powerful canine claws. Within seconds, the cats were all rushing to get through the gates. Satan himself only just scrambled through in time, as the dogs stretched up the ironwork on their hind legs, snapping viciously, or hovered, flicking their bat-like wings violently.

Once outside, Satan faced them defiantly (knowing they could not leave the grounds) and paced up and down, taunting them. (Though in truth, his stomach was taut with fear and his paws severely shaking.) Eventually, having dismissed his pride back to their quarters, he turned, and strutted to the Verger's lodge to lick his wounds. The Scoobies flew back to their posts, and began grooming themselves like birds of prey, after a kill.

CHAPTER 6 — LOCKDOWN, LOCKED IN

Below ground, in the soundproofed quarters of the Guardians, the corridors were in silence – all blissfully unaware of the fracas above. All were in their rooms praying.

Alison preferred to stand to pray, as she did to sing. She was facing the long mirror on her wardrobe, to check her posture was correct, and then had closed her eyes and opened her hands in expectation. *You never know what the Maker will give* she'd regularly told her students. Behind her, on her piano, a metronome swung to and fro, guiding how long each breath grew, paused, and emptied.

Next door, between several large drums, Hikaru was kneeling on a rug, his head bowed, reverencing two Japanese drumsticks laid in the shape of a cross. He was completely still, yet actively sensing and slowing his breathing.

Further along, Gustav was reclining on an enormous blue bean bag covered in miniature cartoon figures of Notre Dame Cathedral topped with a smiling *Mousimodo*. He was holding his fingers to his forehead in concentration. Gently he inhaled the aroma of freshly ground coffee, held it, then let it go, timed beautifully by the rhythmic *whoosh* of his Parisien percolator.

In the next room, Molly sat at her desk; her walls plastered with large sheets of tracing paper (her technical drawings), everything from her earliest designs for chairicopters to her recent robotic mouse-sweeper. She leant forward, her elbows supporting her hands, mirrored together in prayer. She too was breathing like the others, but for her, to the tick of a mechanised cuckoo-clock.

Then, just before Edmund's, came Nathanael's, the Infirmarian, with a large diagram of the internal organs of mice marking his door. (Marcus again had received several complaints about it, because it turned many Guardians' stomachs on the way to dinner!) Fortunately, as Nat was chair of S.M.E.C. (Sacrimouse Medical Ethics Council) there was also one of their large posters: *BAN EXPERIMENTATION ON SHALLOWNESSIANS,* which many pinned over the worst bits of his diagram, whenever they could. As a local lad, Nat's walls were covered in prints of Old Corliol, his framed *University of Combria Medical Degree* lost within them. He sat upright in a revolving office chair, the fingers of his right hand feeling the pulse on his left wrist. He counted slowly in his beloved Cumbrian: *yan, tyan, tethera,* as he breathed in, then held it; and breathed out: *methera, pimp.*

Edmund though was just sitting on his bed, struggling. He had always found it hard to keep still, and always preferred to keep active: to pray and walk or pray and clean.

'As long as you're ready to listen as well as talk,'his old guardian mentor had said, 'You don't always have to be physically still. You need to develop as many ways of entering the *Exchange* as you can.'

Well, he'd tried; and managed it quite well at services when the others were there – but keeping still and tuning-in to the *Exchange* when he was alone or worried? THAT was impossible. He paced up and down his bedroom a couple of times but then gave in, *there must be a clue to where she'd gone,* he thought. Then, before he had really decided, he found his paws delicately opening his door, his snout and eyes checking the way ahead, and his feet tiptoeing towards Jan's room.

Edmund inched his way along the corridor with his back against the wall, flicking his head this-way-and-that, pausing to listen for footsteps. He passed Nathanael's, Gustav's, Molly's, then Hikaru's room with its large circular leopard skin mounted upon it (the rules allowed each guardian one personal possession to be displayed on their door). Then he reached Alison's (plastered with various *Queen* albums – which had originally left the Prior a little disconcerted, especially when he saw tracks like *It's a Hard Life* and *I Want to Break Free*). He had nearly reached Jan's, when he heard the lift 'ping'.

'Great Tolfink!' He gasped, 'Everyone's supposed to be in their rooms!'

He managed to dodge behind the benches in the lobby just as the lift doors opened.

'SShh… just move slowly,' came a voice.

From where he was lying, Edmund could only see a pair of feet, then suddenly, two more following.

'We're doing ok,' came the voice again, 'we've just got to get it to the pick-up point and hope tonight's brew won't be quite as fizzy!'

The two other mice made no comment, except for gasping a little, as if they were pushing something heavy, on what looked like a couple of Sam's skateboards? The feet soon shuffled towards the Dining Room. Edmund listened for movement and then raised his head. *Gone, good!*

Quickly he dashed towards Jan's door, and leapt through it, opening and closing it in one smooth movement. He stood bolt upright, his back and hands against the door, panting more out of fear than physical exertion. He listened intently *Nothing, good.* He switched on the light. *There must be a clue somewhere*, he thought.

He looked under her bed – just a pink suitcase covered in flight stickers – he knew she was often away, but hadn't realised the extent of her trips: *Mouscow*, *Mousal* in Iraq, *Disneyland*? *How did she manage that?* He felt the lamp on her bedside table for heat, then realised it had an LED bulb, so it would never get warm anyway (The Guardians were very committed to reducing their carbon footprint – though being mice, it wasn't that big anyway). *No telling if she'd been back then, or how recently she had left,* he surmised. In the corner, on the shelf above the sink, were the usual toothbrush, soaps, and a very nice bottle of *Mousnifique* by *Loncôme*. The only place left to look was the wardrobe.

Edmund was unsure whether he wanted to open it – just in case the horrible truth was lurking within. He sniffed it first, but all he picked up was a hint of perfume. He consoled himself that, since they had never found Peter's body, it was more than likely that Jan's was buried elsewhere too. Timorously he pulled the wardrobe doors open and there before him was…

…a very ordinary wardrobe!

Well, that wasn't quite true. Jan's wardrobe seemed twice as big as everyone else's – certainly bigger than his. Moreover, despite the usual shelves and coat rails, Jan had her own pull-cord right at the back as well! *Very posh* he mused, *I guess a bit more light wouldn't harm;* and reaching out, he gave the cord a quick tug.

Suddenly the doors closed behind him, he was bathed in red light and a dispassionate female voice announced:

'You have ten seconds to complete the password; He will give his angels charge over you.'

Edmund froze.

'Nine, eight,' she counted, then added, as if out of courtesy, 'six seconds remaining before incineration.'

'Incineration?!' Edmund panicked.

He could see the light above him growing in intensity like a red-hot laser, and he could imagine the pile of dust on the floor afterwards: a jigsaw of tiny bones, like the leftovers of a fried chicken takeaway. All he could think of was the second half of the scripture!

'Two.'

'To... to... keep you in all your ways!' he stammered.

'One.'

Edmund screwed his eyes shut and grabbed the wall unit to steady himself for the blast. To Edmund's relief, nothing happened; instead, the whole wall spun around, and he found himself in a room surrounded by monitors.

'What the...?' he exclaimed.

The female voice returned, 'All systems active. You have two messages.'

Edmund didn't know where to look. He knew Jan was someone special, but he had no idea she was involved in anything like this. Before him stood a central touch-screen table that had five large icons on its screen, four on the top and one below them. The first icon was *Mice Intelligence 5*, the next *Mice Intelligence 6*, then came *Admiralty Mouse*, and *MCHQ*. The one below just read *Pizza domine*.

I must tell the Prior, Edmund resolved. But as he turned to leave the room, the wall held firm. He pushed against it, shoulder-charged it and even kicked it, but it refused to move. He scoured the room for some switch or button, but there was no pull-cord on the inside. By now he was sweating profusely: *how could he get a message to the Prior? How would he explain himself to Jan on her return? What if she didn't return? He could be stuck there for days, weeks even!* He began pacing the room in panic.

'Help! Help!' he called, banging on the wall; but he knew their rooms, carved out of earth, were pretty soundproof. There was a sort of vent in the ceiling, the shape of a large letterbox, so he realised he'd be all right for air.

In the corner was a plumbed-in hamster water bottle, so he knew he could drink. *But what about food? While she jetted off across the world, would he be left to starve? Or worse... what if she really had gone the way of Peter? He might NEVER be found!*

CHAPTER 7 — STARRY NIGHT

'Come on, wake up,' a voice commanded.

But as Robbie came round, all he could see was deeper darkness, and all he could hear was a caterwauling from outside.

'Don't worry,' Jan explained, 'the cats must have tried to force the doors.'

'And?'

'Oh. And the sentinels would have been activated.'

Robbie opened his arms in a quizzical gesture, and with some exasperation.

'Sentinels?'

'The Scoobies,' Jan explained. 'The stone gargoyles shaped like dogs on the tower. They guard the entrance doors and activate if any felines try and break in.'

'What?' Robbie argued, 'You ARE kidding me. I've been here tons and I've never seen any *Scoobies*!' he laughed.

'Seeing is believing, hey?' she questioned. 'But didn't you hear them?'

Robbie had to admit the noise DID sound like a load of dogs fighting with a load of cats.

Jan was becoming more frustrated.

'You Shallownessians put evidence and explanation before experience. Just because you can't explain something, doesn't mean it's not real! You struggle to believe that some stone figures can come alive, yet you seem to have forgotten you've apparently just witnessed a load of talking cats and been led by a talking mouse through stone walls, without using a door!'

Robbie accepted she had a point; but more importantly, he wanted to know what all this star business was about. He eventually plucked up courage to ask.

'They want to steal a star?'

Jan thought hard. *Should I tell the annoying little Shallownessian? No, I'll show him, that will blow his mind.*

Jan turned away, pretending to ignore him.

'Torch,' she instructed, 'use your phone.'

Robbie was still gripping it in his hand, and dutifully he switched it on. Bit by bit, his eyes focused, first on Jan, then on the high roof above them, then the ancient stone walls, and finally right before him, ironwork, covering what he later discovered was an old well.

'So, we really are…?'

'Yes,' dismissed Jan, 'we're inside the Temple.'

'So we have…'

'Yes, passed through solid walls,' interrupted Jan, 'the stone arch is our portal in, and this well, our portal out.'

Robbie was not just impressed, but more than a little excited. *Well-good,* he smiled; but as he reached for his night-sight goggles, he felt a sharp nip on his ear.

'Ow!'

He grabbed it, checking for blood.

'I think we've finished with those,' whispered Jan, 'don't you?'

'You didn't need to bite me!' Robbie protested,

'Oh, for heaven's sake!' Jan retorted, 'Are you a man or a mouse?!'

Robbie didn't get the irony.

'Anyway,' she continued, 'we don't bite, we nibble! And one day, Master Robbie, you'll be glad of a female who will…,' Jan stopped and thought better of continuing.

Robbie just sat there, constantly checking his ear lobe, and trying to find enough light to take a selfie.

'You're fine, you're fine,' assured Jan impatiently, 'now can we please move on?'

Robbie refused to look at her, huffed, and shone his phone around. He caught something on the far wall, by the entrance doors – a stone plaque covered in chiseled shapes.

'What's that?' he questioned.

'What?' Jan grumbled.

'THAT!' Robbie pointed to where he was shining: the large stone engraved with curious letters and symbols.

'Oh, that,' Jan sighed, disinterested. 'That's Old Norse – what the Vikings spoke.'

'Vikings? Woah! What's it doing there? What does it say?' *This is mega*, grinned Robbie.

Jan was not as enthusiastic. 'It's just one of the first stones they must have laid when they built the Temple,' she explained. 'They're what we call runes – secret symbols.'

Robbie strode over to it, crouched down and began outlining each symbol with his fingers. He read aloud the translation above it.

'I Tolfink wrote these runes on this stone. Who's Tolfink?'

'Heaven knows. Possibly one of the first masons, I don't know,' Jan dismissed.

Robbie wouldn't let go, 'But why did he write it?'

Jan was becoming more annoyed, 'I don't know, I guess he just wanted to put his mark on it! Maybe because he'd made it. Like signing a painting or making your mark like the other masons have?'

(Robbie had noticed their individual signatures, some simple, some ornate, all over the cathedral pillars and walls.)

'He must have been proud of his work to mark it,' added Robbie – who had never considered anything HE had made was that good.

Jan suddenly felt sorry for him.

'You're right. You only put your mark on something you think is good, or beautiful or wonderful. Why do you think the Maker has put his mark, his image, on us?'

Robbie fell silent.

Jan gave him a few moments to take it in then gently coaxed: 'Shall we move on?'

Robbie, distractedly, complied and followed where Jan was pointing. The beam of his torch hit a wooden archway, then moved upwards revealing gigantic organ pipes that stood at attention, like a row of silent guardsmen outside a royal palace.

'This way,' she commanded, hopping towards, then through, the arch. In the deep darkness Robbie stopped; then gasped in wonder.

The rich azure ceiling was shimmering in a curious light – its own light! It was alive: not just with stars, but with planets of various sizes, shooting all over the place – like a planetarium on e-numbers! Heavenly bodies were hurtling around the angels on the roof beams, around the canons' stalls, around the brass eagle, and around HIM! He felt the chilled breeze of their zooming on his face and hands as they passed. He ducked as their buzz and whoosh skirted his head and gasped as they changed colours and brightness, refracting the light.

'Close your mouth for goodness' sake,' chided Jan, 'haven't you seen a Milky Way before?'

'Not like this!' Robbie blurted, exploding with excitement.

He wasn't sure how long he had stood there mesmerised by the planets and suns but eventually stuttered: 'What, what are they doing?'

Jan sighed, 'Energising of course.'

'Energising?'

'You don't think everything runs by itself, do you? What do you think Temples are for? How could the Maker power the world without Pumping Stations?'

'So, you make energy?'

'No, no, no, we just channel it, for the Maker.'

'I'm not with you.'

'Well, you don't think we sing for the good of our own health, do you? The Maker longs to energise the world, but he needs channels through which to pump his life. It's not just us you know – anyone can be a channel for him.'

Robbie couldn't take his eyes off the stars before him. He'd seen constellations before, but not shooting around like this. He blinked, then closed his eyes for a second, almost wishing it to be a trick. Finally, all he could say was: 'Wow. It's... it's... beautiful!'

At last Jan smiled. 'Of course it is,' she emphasised, 'the Maker never makes anything less! Our whole worlds overflow with beauty, and life, and love. Think of the vastness and colours of the plants and animals and skies and seas. Think of the millions of people. Then think of the billions of galaxies and stars and worlds we don't even know about! The Maker has given us so much. Yet you Shallownessians take it all so lightly. You ignore the way you poison it all. I'm sorry, but you're more like cats than us! Why can't you just *still* yourselves, breathe it all in, and treasure it?'

It was all too much for Robbie. This *Maker* business was beginning to change the way he looked at HIS world, never mind theirs!

'And that's the *Exchange*?' he finally asked.

'Absolutely. When we are still or sing to the Maker,' she thought for a moment, 'it's like the sun coming out on a rainy day: the earth is warmed, the flowers open, our hearts too are changed.'

Robbie wasn't quite convinced but WAS finding it interesting, especially when she spoke about the stars and universe (or multiverse?).

'Look, see those large pipes, the organ pipes if you want to call them that. Well, when we sing, they suck in the hurt and pain in the world and channel it up to the Maker. On the next breath, they suck down energy from the Maker, and channel it out to the world. It's not rocket science, the Maker powers everything, even you and me.'

Robbie thought for a minute. 'So, it's a sort of machine?'

'Certainly not! You Shallownessians always see things as mechanical, don't you? Something that YOU'VE made, and YOU control. No, no, no, the Exchange is more ancient than that. Like I said, it's alive! More, what would you say? An organism; yes, more an organism than a machine, why do you think they call them organs?'

Robbie was even more confused. Just then, a planet the size of a golf ball headed straight for him. Before he had time to move out the way it reached his face, stopping millimetres from his nose. Robbie took a sharp intake of breath and went cross-eyed as he stared at it; but within a millisecond it let out an enormous squeal and sent a shock wave through the air – gathering planets as it went. A second later, all the planets had been absorbed back into their stars on the ceiling as if nothing had happened.

'Oh no,' said Robbie, 'they've stopped, I've ruined everything!'

Jan laughed. 'Of course, you haven't. They can run the exchange from up there just as well: that's what they do for the Canons on the dayshift, and for us during our services. It's just, when we've finished, they like to get out a bit.'

Robbie again, was unconvinced.

'Remember, they're not MAKING energy, just channeling it, and the best way to do that, is just to be still, and 'open'.'

Robbie still looked puzzled. 'And anyone can do this?'

'Anyone. You just have to calm yourself, breathe slowly in, hold for a few seconds, then breathe slowly out – you'll be amazed at what happens.'

'Maybe for you weird mice, you Guardians,' Robbie dismissed, 'but not for us.'

'The Canons can do it,' argued Jan, 'and some Shallownessians we know can.'

'Well, they must be weird too,' Robbie concluded.

Jan thought for a moment.

'Tell me Robbie, have you ever held a starfish?'

'Once, when I was little.'

'I'm impressed, which beach were you on?'

'Oh, it wasn't outside, it was in an aquarium.'

'Oh,' responded Jan disappointed, then quickly added, 'what did it feel like?'

'Bit weird, sort of leathery on the top and tickly on the bottom.'

'But you liked it?'

'Not really, it didn't DO anything.'

'I see. Would you be surprised if I told you that a starfish, or, as some call it, a *sea star*, is as important to the Maker as a real star?'

Robbie smiled mockingly, 'Really?'

'No, seriously,' countered Jan, 'you see, life isn't about how big you are or how much you can do; but about how intricately made, how unique you are. The Maker doesn't duplicate anything, every living thing is special to him – a unique project – and, therefore, never exactly the same.'

Robbie thought for a minute. 'What about identical twins then?' he challenged.

Jan smiled, thinking of Ben and Sam: 'Living things often share characteristics, often look the same, but each twin is unique.' Jan sighed, 'Look, shine your phone on the canons' seats.'

Robbie did so.

'They all look the same, don't they?'

Robbie nodded.

'But the wood carvers, because they believed every canon was unique, decorated every stall differently, giving each a unique carving under their seat. Even today, whoever is made a canon, is reminded of this, by being given a unique stall, their own number too, which no-one else is allowed to sit in.'

'So?'

'They are all assured they are special, all shown that the Maker loves them just for who they are, not for what they can do. And what's more, their hearts will never be at rest, never be fully alive, until they rest in that love, rest in him.'

Robbie looked none the wiser. To be honest, he felt more comfortable discussing talking cats and flying planets than this *Maker* gadgee!

'Come on,' surrendered Jan, tugging his collar, 'this way. Oh, better switch your torch on, it gets dark down here. We have to report to the bishop.'

CHAPTER 8 — AN AUDIENCE WITH THE BISHOP

Jan led Robbie past an enormous chair (which apparently belonged to the bishop). Robbie pulled a face in shock: *Flipping 'eck, how big is this guy?*

She led him down some steps into a darkened aisle covered in brass and marble plaques. Jan saw him straining to look at them.

'Just in memory of Shallownessian canons,' she dismissed. 'Keep ahead towards the corner over there.'

As they neared the end of the aisle, Robbie saw a decorative stone portico (similar to the one his dad used to pore over when he was dragged to the garden centre at Dolston). But this one bore a couple of figures, or rather heads, above it.

Jan called out: 'Bishop Jim; My Lord Bishop!'

Suddenly one of the stone heads, with a bejewelled hat, replied.

'For goodness' sake, can't anyone sleep around here.'

Robbie didn't know what to say, but then the next head, some sort of King with a crown, spoke more gently: 'Don't be so miserable,' he retorted, 'you've been sleeping all day! Anyway, you should be glad of the company.'

'Well, it's better than yours I suppose,' said the rich man.

'I'd ignore him,' said the king. 'He's always in a bad mood. Now how can we help?'

'We're trying to see the bishop, your majesty,' proffered Jan.

'Hah,' replied the king, 'you'll be lucky, spends most of his time sleeping nowadays. But if you want to try, hop up onto me, and see if you can rouse him.'

Gratefully Jan leapt from Robbie's shoulder and took up position on the King's crown, then peered into the corner.

'My Lord Bishop!' she called.

Robbie moved closer and to his astonishment, he could make out a third head skulking in the corner. It was indeed a bishop (Robbie recognised the pointy hat he was wearing), but this bishop looked asleep, very asleep, and disappointingly small.

Jan called again.

The bishop snaffled and snored, but his eyes remained quite shut. Jan gently but purposefully scratched the bishop on his nose, and he woke with startled eyes, and automatically broke out into a chant.

'Our hearts are restless till they rest in you,' then he shook himself alert. 'What the devil?' he burst, peering at Jan. Then, frowning at Robbie added, 'And what's HE doing here?'

'He's with me,' explained Jan, confidently.

'But can we trust him?' continued the bishop, inquisitively.

'I think so,' countered Jan.

The bishop squinted at Robbie for a second, then seemed to capitulate.

'All right then, what's going on?'

'Well,' said Jan, 'we have a sort of crisis.'

'Come on then,' encouraged the bishop, 'spit it out.'

Jan, still lithe for her age, leapt from the crown to the mitre (the bishop's hat), crept down his head and began whispering in his ear. Robbie moved closer.

'Oh dear,' muttered the bishop. 'Oh, dearie me,' continued the bishop. 'Oh hell!' he finally concluded, 'I quite see your predicament. You must act at once. You know what to do!'

Jan visibly gulped, and for the first time since he'd met her, Robbie could tell she was scared.

'Brief Prior Marcus immediately.'

'As you wish, my Lord,' she replied.

'May the Maker go with you!' called the bishop.

'Thank you, my Lord,' Jan replied, bowing reverently.

With that, she leapt back onto the crown, thanked his majesty, then bounded back onto Robbie's shoulder.

'Good luck!' added the King, 'sounds frightfully exciting!'

'Good riddance!' grumped the rich man.

Jan was deep in thought… 'This way,' she commanded.

Robbie obediently made his way back up the aisle, asking; 'Well? What did he say?'

'It's not good, Robbie. Satan has been growing his pride and is determined to steal a star.'

'Is that bad?'

'No, it's disastrous! Our whole existence is at stake!'

Robbie cocked his head to one side as if willing her to go on. Jan continued.

'Ok. I'll be frank. We are not called *guardians* for nothing. The Exchange, which the canons built, is reasonably safe from Shallownessians; to them it is just gold stars on a blue ceiling, and the organ just a musical instrument. OUR problem is the felines. Like us, their forebears came over with the French canons and accidentally listened-in to the song of the Maker. Like us they learnt how to become still, opening their hearts, and over centuries, like us they began to change. The result was, as we desired the Maker's love, and so were given the Maker's image – human faces – THEY desired the Maker's power; and so, although gaining speech, remained cats, but with unnatural size and strength.'

Robbie froze. Just when he thought there couldn't be anything more – a whole additional world was emerging.

Jan continued, 'Like the canons above, we too devoted ourselves to the exchange and became known as *sacrimice* – rodents bearing the Maker's image. A few of the *mundomice* (what we call your house mice), joined us, but most drove us out, so we had to build our own villages. Several of us chose to devote ourselves to the Maker's song and became night-shift canons.

'We mirrored the canons' buildings below ground: constructing our own quarters under the Temple and our own village under theirs. The first few centuries were hell. The felines were living with the Shallownessians and controlled the whole grounds. They soon recognised how special the stars were and made several attempts to steal one. That was when we were renamed Guardians. Then, because the canons kept adding buildings, the Shallownessian village had to move out – and the felines and mundomice went with them. It wasn't long before our village followed – leaving only us on site.'

'So, there's a whole village of you somewhere?'

Jan laughed, 'Not just here Robbie. We have villages all over the world, usually near a Temple – so they can supply the guardians. Where else would we get new guardians from?'

Robbie didn't think he could take much more. Having a few talking mice was one thing, but having a whole family of them across the world? Surely not.

'So, there's a village near here?' he pressed.

'Underneath the church at Borgh-by-Sands,' she replied, nonchalantly. 'They have a nearby dairy, and deliver milk for our Creamery, and we pay them back in cheese. We use the black bin by Vernon's lodge as our drop-off point.'

Robbie just stood there astounded. It was the way she treated it all as matter of fact that shocked him most. He still didn't quite understand. Even if they lost a star, it wouldn't be a disaster, would it?

Jan shot her face towards him and spoke more sharply than he had ever heard her before.

'Don't you get it? Each star is unique, bringing a unique offer to the Exchange – without just one we would be so much less. Stealing a star is what the felines live for. With a star or two they aim to build their own exchange – growing power, not love!'

Robbie had had enough. He was certain he hadn't asked that aloud – yet she had answered.

'You can read minds, can't you?' he accused.

Jan started to blush.

'I would have told you eventually,' she apologised. 'Shallownessian brains are pretty easy. Felines are pretty resistant unfortunately.'

Robbie wasn't sure what he felt. Just when he thought he had made a good friend, whom he could trust, it turned out she'd been holding back her ability to read his every thought.

'I AM sorry,' she stressed.

Robbie held back a tear. He was angry as much as disappointed. *Could he not trust anyone? Surely someone would have seen the guardians at some time? Why had no-one told him about it before?*

Jan couldn't help answering, 'Jim, the bishop, saw us once. He was so bent on connecting with us that we let him in on our mission. From then on, he secretly recruited *Woke* Shallownessians to aid us. They are known as *Stellarii*. It was one of them I was supposed to meet tonight.'

Robbie suddenly snapped out of his hurt. 'Wicked!' he gasped. *There are humans helping them.* 'Can I meet one?'

'Out of the question!' she replied. 'Firstly, because their identities need to remain completely hidden, in case they are forced to disclose another (imagine being exposed as someone who believes in humanoid mice and killer cats! They would never work again, they'd lose everything!). Secondly, for the same reason, we, the agents of Corliol, don't know who they are either (they always cover their face when we meet, again for protection). All I know is, they have really helped us in the past, and we hope they will, in the future.'

Robbie's night was exploding with excitement. He felt on top of the world – both worlds! Discovering there were sacrimice as well as normal mice, and mutant felines as well as normal cats were nothing to NOW finding out his cathedral was at the centre of a power struggle, with real stars at risk of being stolen! He wanted to sing, he wanted to jump, THIS was becoming the best night ever of his life!

That was his second mistake.

CHAPTER 9 — A FORTUNATE ESCAPE

As Jan neared the crossing Robbie saw a figure to his right muttering under his breath.

'Who's that?' he whispered.

'Oh, he's one of the more recent deans.'

'Why is he lying down? Are all deans and bishops sleepy?'

''Fraid so,' agreed Jan.

'Really?'

'Of course not,' she corrected, 'they just sculpt them lying down to show they're at rest.'

Robbie scanned the white marble figure. 'He's holding a book,' noticed Robbie, 'a bible?'

'For goodness' sake,' said Jan, 'I suppose so, why don't you go and ask him?'

'What?'

'ASK him. Haven't you got it yet? The Temple's alive at night: gargoyles, the stars, the statues.'

'But you said we had to rush back?'

'Ah, I see. Though the Temple stays active, we guardians always close the portal an hour or so after we finish our worship – otherwise we'd have to stay up all night guarding it.'

I guess it makes sense, thought Robbie.

Jan quickly replied, 'Look, try not to understand everything – just enjoy experiencing it.'

But I'm not wired like that, Robbie insisted. *It's a whole new world – everything is different. There are different rules at play, different priorities, a different way of life – it's all upside down – all this giving rather than getting, letting go rather than controlling.* Although it all felt so mystifying, Robbie had to admit, it also felt exhilarating: whole new worlds were becoming real to him: and possibly his own too? *What if you weren't valued for what you could do – but simply for who you were – scars and all?*

Jan, listening in, gave him a thumbs up. 'Be patient,' she advised, then added excitedly, 'you ARE getting there you know!'

Emboldened, Robbie marched up to the sleeping figure.

''Scuse me sir,'

'Dean,' came the reply.

''Scuse me dean sir, what are you reading?'

The dean came round with a cough.

'Ah, a fellow Shallownessian,' he replied learnedly, 'what can I do for you?'

'I was wondering…'

'Oh yes,' said the dean, 'wondering is very good, never be afraid to wonder, young man.'

'Sorry, I meant, I was wondering what that book was, in your hand?'

'Ahh, curious too, excellent. Well now young…young?'

'Robbie.'

'What would you think I'd be reading?'

Ooh thought Robbie, 'I have no idea.'

'Come on now,' taunted the dean jestingly, 'you can narrow it down to Greek or Latin or Mathematics, can't you?'

Not knowing any books in Greek or Latin or on Maths, Robbie hesitantly offered: 'The Bible?'

'Hah,' the dean broke out in a roar of laughter. 'The Bible… The Bible!' he kept repeating, chuckling to himself, 'That's a good one! The sculptor shaped it well didn't he, just the *cover* I needed… If you, what is it you young'uns say, *get my drift, bro.*'

Robbie looked puzzled, 'Drift?'

'Ah, you young'uns forget we hear everything you say on your e-phones: OMG!'

Robbie grimaced, *was this guy for real*? He quickly got the dean back on topic.

'So, it's not The Bible?'

'No, no, no, no,' breathed the dean, then victoriously proclaimed 'LOL,' and burst out laughing, ending up dabbing the tears from his eyes with his lacey cuffs. Then, gasping for breath, he continued, almost in pain, 'Oh, oh, my dear boy, it may look like a bible, but I assure you it isn't.'

'Then what is it?' probed Robbie, becoming a little tired.

Struggling to speak, the dean panted, 'It's, it's Winnie ille pu.'

'You what?'

'Oh,' the dean giggled, 'Em… em,' and winking, whispered, 'FYI, to you it will be *Winnie the Pooh* – but this translation is in the original Latin.'

Load of nonsense judged Robbie. He didn't know much about books and stuff, but he knew for certain the novel hadn't been around for much more than a hundred years. He'd seen the film too – and it certainly wasn't Roman!

But before Robbie could press further, Jan had run up his back and pulled rather heavily on his collar.

'Sorry Frank,' she addressed the dean, 'we've gotta go.'

'Oh, very well,' he capitulated, still giggling, 'BFN. A bible, a bible, oh dear, dear,' they could hear him chortling as they moved on down the aisle.

'Are all deans that crazy?' asked Robbie.

'Pretty much so,' sighed Jan, 'it comes with the job!' Suddenly she tugged Robbie's collar again: 'Stop!'

'What?'

Jan sniffed the air. 'Felines! No, wait… oh no… quick, hide!' She ushered him back towards the sleeping dean. 'Quick, behind the curtains!'

Robbie speedily climbed on top of the ledge and slid behind some velvet curtains. Jan quickly scampered on top of Harvey, one of the bishops, his fingertips resting together in prayer.

'Ooh that tickles,' he giggled.

'Shh,' whispered Jan, 'please Harvey, we need to hide!'

'Oh, ok,' replied the bishop in disappointment, as Jan tucked herself in behind his ear.

There was a heavy thud as the key in the main door clunked, echoing down the aisle. Then there came the 'beep- beep- beeping' of the alarm, as a human tapped in the code. Both Jan and Robbie held their breath as a bright light stretched down the aisle towards them: accompanied by some heavy, slow, footsteps. *Vernon the Verger!* Jan recognised.

Sure enough, as the light progressed, a rather large figure plodded past her hiding place. Vernon seemed to be whispering to someone, and it was only then that she not only saw the large torch in his right hand, but the large cat tucked under his left. *Satan! So that's how he's been getting in!* she thought aloud.

Vernon paused. In the dim light falling from the windows, you could make out his bull-like shape, fat round head and the broadest shoulders you could imagine.

‘I knows you’re in ‘ere,’ he called into the darkness, searching the walls with his light. ‘And the police are on their way. Give yourselves up now, while you can.’

Robbie detected a London or southern accent. Indeed, Vernon was an Essex boy, *joined the army at twenty,* he used to say, *dishonourably discharged at thirty*, (apparently some mix up about some bottles of whiskey and the officers’ mess). He’d then joined the wrong sort and ended up in prison for five years, where he’d discovered a talent for weightlifting, cage-fighting and needlework. He’d subsequently had a change of heart, and finally got a job at the cathedral – to some people’s alarm – repairing the vestments. (The Dean had insisted they must accept him quoting the rules of their community written by their founder St. Gus: *hate the sin but love the sinner,* and the canons had succumbed.) Eventually, the Dean appointed him to head caretaker (or verger).

Although he was completely reformed, one glimpse of his fingers, with the letters H.A.T.E. on the knuckles of one hand, and H.A.T.E., on the other, said it all. (He’d been told by the tattooist it was fifteen pounds a word, so he had argued he shouldn’t have to pay again if the same word was used on his other hand.) Though to the regular churchgoers it had been a little off-putting; there was never any trouble during the services, or as the Dean put it, ‘No love lost, because there was no L.O.V.E in the first place.’

As he drew near, Jan herself turned to prayer. *Please, please, please*, she begged, breathing in slowly, holding, then breathing out even slower. She hummed the song in her head.

Fortunately, Vernon stopped with his back to the curtains and inspected the windows instead. 'No sign of forced entry,' he murmured. 'Maybe we *was* wrong, after all, the alarm *'asn't* gone off. I could have sworn I heard dogs or *summat.* Maybe those pesky mice, huh! Better not have messed up me marble, I haven't time to polish it again tomorrow.'

Vernon inspected the floor with his torch – *no sign of any damage*. He was just about to leave when Satan began to wriggle and then leapt onto the ledge where Robbie was hiding.

Robbie stiffened in panic. He could see the cat through a worn hole in the fabric and was desperately trying to breathe naturally.

Satan stretched and sniffed the air, then started rubbing his behind on the curtains and spraying his scent. He stalked nearer and nearer.

Robbie closed his eyes pretending it wasn't happening, then gasped in horror, as he glanced down, and realised the toes of his boots were clearly peeping out below the curtain. All at once his nostrils set on fire, his throat turned to sand and his chest ignited.

'Great Tolfink!' Jan exploded, knowing the game was up. Bravely she leapt from Frank and whispered loudly: 'Oi yer useless ball of fur, I'm over here!'

In a flash, Satan turned and dived from the ledge in a rage.

Jan dashed down the aisle towards the well and had nearly reached the ironwork when Satan made an enormous leap, his arms stretched rigid, his talons stretched wide, and his mouth stretched open – before crashing into the grill: legs, head, mouth, splattering against its unforgiving steel.

'Ahhhh!' he squealed. Then, in his fury he forced his right paw through the metalwork, feeling frantically for Jan's panting body – but she had squeezed herself up onto a shelf just under the bars, and he searched in vain.

'Come on ye daft cat,' shouted Vernon, 'what you doing? Check down 'ere for me.'

Trying to hide his embarrassment (and his pain), Satan scowled into the darkness.

'Come on!' shouted Vernon.

'Next time,' the cat whispered, as he reluctantly retracted his claws and trotted off to his master.

Jan waited and let out a huge breath.

When she was convinced Vernon's muttering was some distance away, she crept back to the ledge. 'Psst, psst,' she whispered, 'time to go!'

Robbie crept down.

'Quick, the door,' she ordered, but Robbie froze.

'But what about you?' he asked.

'Just GO home.'

'But I want to help. I want to be a *Stellarii*!'

Jan sighed; *he had been useful – a little?* 'Ok then, but no promises, come back tonight.'

'What time?'

Jan thought for a minute, 'Let's say one a.m.'

'Well-good,' Robbie squealed, and couldn't help skipping to the doors. But as he glanced back, Jan, who had been standing near the entrance to the organ arch, miles from a heating grill or the well, had completely disappeared.

How did she do that? thought Robbie.

On hearing the huffing of Vernon and Satan approaching, he quickly dashed out the door, and stepped outside into the warm air.

How come it's warmer out here than in there? Robbie thought, then shrugged and sprinted home.

CHAPTER 10 — A WELCOME RETURN, BUT NOT OF ALL

It took Edmund a few seconds to come round and realise he was still trapped in Jan's control room. He gratefully drank some water, and again began to feel the walls for some sort of secret button. After an hour or so, he went back to the control screen. *There's nothing for it*, he decided, *I'll have to try and contact MI5 or something.* He studied the different icons, took a deep breath, *here goes* he risked, and pressed the MI5 icon. The screen flashed, and a box appeared labelled 'password?'

Edmund sighed, 'Useless!'

He pressed MI6 and that too asked for a password. He tried all the top line: all password protected. Then he thought: if he could just get through to Pizza Domine, maybe he could get a message to Marcus? *THIS better not be password protected as well*, he grumped.

To his relief, the box that appeared was just plain – no mention of any password. Edmund's face lit up and he quickly typed: *Help! locked in Jan's secret room, Temple 2am,* and pressed 'send'.

Another box appeared: *Please press to add the following: extra cheese, garlic bread, coleslaw, mayonnaise, French fries.*

Edmund pressed them all. Another box appeared: *Thank you, Jan, your Pizza Domine order has been received and added to your account. Thank you for ordering from Pizza Domine, the best micero-meals south of the border.*

'And?' voiced Edmund, 'And? Have you got that I'm trapped?'

The box disappeared.

'Useless!' Edmund gasped. Then resolved to try again. *Perhaps they'd query a second order and get in touch?* Determined, he began the order process all over again.

#

Jan wasted no time in catching a lift down to their quarters. She dashed along the corridor, hurtled through the kitchen, and reached the grotto in record time! Squeezing between the cheeses she activated the secret opening, carelessly crossed the tunnel, and clambered up the ladder. Within minutes she was scrambling up the stairs to the Prior's room.

Marcus and Lesley were sitting by the fireplace talking quietly.

'How's things?' she began as she squeezed through the door.

'Jan, Jan!' They rejoiced, delighted on her safe return. But they were soon troubled by her report... Marcus, however, couldn't contain his joy.

'This calls for a celebration!' he proclaimed, then mysteriously pattered over to the wood panelling beside the fireplace, leant against it, and to their shock, disappeared!

Almost immediately, he reappeared with a dusty bottle of *Special Reserve Dandelion and Burdock.* Lesley and Jan applauded in anticipation; and before long, all three were sipping away (rather noisily according to a bad-tempered Pelican above them). It wasn't long, however, before they had succumbed to its delights and drifted off to sleep.

#

It was well into the morning when they came around and the seriousness of their predicament returned to them. They were concerned that so many felines had been in their grounds, that Satan had such easy access to their Temple, and that cats had also been snooping around their secret access to the Dean's Keep. Marcus formed a triangle with his fingers and held them to his mouth pensively.

'We need to regain control,' suggested Jan.

Marcus nodded but said nothing. A few moments later he sighed and said, 'First things first.' He withdrew his pocket-watch. 'Lesley, would you slip back to our quarters and spread the good news that Jan is safe?'

'Sure,' replied Lesley, 'it'll be a pleasure,' but as she rose, she had to reach out to the paneling, to steady herself.

'You ok?' exclaimed Marc and Jan simultaneously.

'Fine – just a little light-headed – that D and B must have been a little stronger than I thought.'

With that, she took a deep breath, slapped her cheeks, and strode confidently to the door.

'And to regain control?' pursued Jan. 'You know there's only one way?'

Marcus placed his head in his hands, 'There's really no other?'

''Fraid not Marcus, the *Knights of Lonercost* are the only solution.'

The Prior locked his paws together, almost in prayer: 'But last time we had them, we had to pay double to get rid of them.'

(The birds on the ceiling had all fallen silent at the mention of the Knights, THEY didn't want them either.)

'I know,' sighed Jan, 'but the felines are controlling everything, and there's no sign of our Shallownessian contact. What if they have him?'

'Or her,' corrected the Prior. 'You're right. We must prepare for the worst, we have no idea how much Peter told them before...,' the Prior took a breath, 'before he...'

'That's precisely why we need the knights!' Jan interrupted, 'we need to take back control of the grounds at least; until we know where we are.'

(The birds nodded thoughtfully.)

'Ok then,' Marcus surrendered, 'but only on a running contract. I don't want them settling in and making a mess of the grounds like they did last time, riding up and down the banks, churning up the lawns, and absolutely no speedway round the cloister!'

'Fine,' agreed Jan, 'I'll tell them they have to set up camp in the hedges and only move into position tonight.'

'Tonight? They're already on their way?' quizzed the Prior.

'I took the liberty of sending a first-class pigeon last night,' admitted Jan, 'they should be here sometime this afternoon.'

'Lord, help us!' sighed the Prior, 'I only hope we can keep control of them this time and avoid the fury of the Shallownessian canons.'

'I've told them to report to you here,' Jan proffered.

Marcus took a deep breath. 'Ok then. I'll tidy up, you go downstairs and prepare the hatch.'

CHAPTER 11 — ESCAPING AN INTRUDER

Robbie loved having breakfast alone. He could eat what he wanted, watch what he wanted, it was bliss. He then heard his dad stirring in the bathroom. Hurriedly he finished all the *chocobix* – and the milk – then wiped down the table, and dutifully took the carton and some cans out to the recycling bin. He put the kettle on, then sat down for the last part of his favourite TV show, *Horrible Mysteries*. Suddenly, a news flash interrupted:

'Police are asking members of the public to be alert and secure all windows and doors at night, after a significant rise in cat burglaries throughout the city. Detective Inspector Nadia Clew of Combria Police is convinced it's the work of the same gang and she spoke to our reporter Dom Roberts earlier.'

'The M.O. is exactly the same in each case, and forensics have matched hair samples from every incident. Unfortunately, we don't have any CCTV footage yet, but it seems the perpetrators are very agile, have vivid ginger hair and are connected in some way to the fish stall in the market. That's all I can say at the moment. We ask the public to be vigilant as there have also been a series of unconnected sneak thefts around the city centre.'

Robbie then heard the stairs creaking as his dad finally surfaced.

'You ok, dad?' Robbie asked, trying to hide his desperation to find out what, if anything, Geoffrey had remembered from the night before. Geoffrey yawned.

'Not really sure,' came the slow reply, as he stared dreamily out of the window.

I'm for it now, thought, Robbie, *He's working out just how long my grounding is going to be. I wish he'd just shout at me and get it over with.* Eventually Robbie found his tongue, plucked up his courage and faced his doom.

'You, you, remember last night?' he stammered.

'What? Why shouldn't I?' Geoff replied, his nose so blocked he sounded like a deep-sea diver moaning through a helmet.

'Noisy, was it?'

'Not particularly, why?'

Robbie's shoulders lowered with relief. *Has he really forgotten it all? The mouse? The singing? The phone call?*

'Did some-ding wake YOU up Robbie?'

Robbie couldn't help but smile. Then quickly added, 'Just a taxi.'

'Never *'eard* it,' Geoffrey explained, 'I *'eard Dutha* next door, I *dink*.'

Robbie suppressed a giggle. *You only dink?* He wanted to reply but thought it best not to risk it.

'Had the best sleep in ages *dough*.' Geoffrey reckoned. He then began to hum the exact chant Jan and he had secreted in his ear.

'Wow!' Laughed Robbie. *I really am off the hook! I must tell Jan!*

Geoffrey reached for a mug from the top cupboard. As he did so, Robbie did a double-take and froze *it can't be!*

'You want a tea, son?'

'Oh,' Robbie delayed, startled, 'yes please!'

But as Geoffrey opened the cupboard again, Robbie got a clear view. There was no doubt. Laid on a pile of saucers was a chunky bedraggled mouse, its small body rising and falling as if asleep. Robbie sat up in panic. Geoffrey opened the fridge below.

'*Dough* milk?' moaned Geoffrey.

'Sorry dad.'

'*Dough* worries, I'll nip to *de* Co-op, I need a paper anyway.'

'Brill!' puffed Robbie unintentionally.

'What?'

'Oh, nothing,' he mused casually.

Geoffrey grabbed a plastic bag from the lower cupboard and strode for the door. Robbie dashed to open it for him – which only served to make Geoffrey more suspicious.

'Are you ok son?' he checked, 'Is there some-*ding* you need to tell me?'

Tell you? Thought Robbie, *Tell you? What, like a humanoid mouse is in the cupboard? A load of mutant cats are freely roaming the city trying to burgle the cathedral? And I'm going to be a Stellarii – a secret agent?*

'Nope.' Robbie smiled.

'Hmm.' Geoffrey frowned, pensively; but opened the door and headed for the back gate. Robbie checked through the kitchen window, then went to the cupboard.

Slowly he pulled it open, and sure enough, still curled on the top saucer was a mouse, in similar clothes to Jan, its body rising and falling with its breath. *Well, it's still alive,* Robbie decided, *and I can't leave it here. But what if this one isn't friendly? What if THIS one bites?* Robbie gingerly took hold of the saucer and slid it off the top. The mouse didn't move.

Keeping the saucer level, he purposefully went to the stairs and began climbing, his eyes fixed on the sleeping creature. *Now, where to hide it?* He entered his bedroom, placed the saucer gently on his desk, and looked around for a hiding place. *Do they like dark places?* he wondered, and *how can I make sure you won't escape?* Then he saw it! His old wooden chess set! Quickly he emptied all the pieces onto his bed and placed the wooden box next to the saucer. *Something soft*, he thought. He raided his sock drawer, scrunched up an old football sock, and placed it inside the box as a mattress. *Right,* he thought, *now the rodent.*

Deliberately he picked up the saucer and began tilting it towards the box, but instead of sliding off into the box, the mouse held firm. Robbie braced himself, and with his other hand, he reached out to the sleeping creature, and gently began to pull it with his finger. Still, it stayed. *Got it,* thought Robbie: and keeping the saucer in position, he lifted up the sock, and cleverly sandwiched the mouse between the two, turning it upside down and lowering it into the box. *I must remember to get it some water,* he thought, *and food.* Quietly Robbie slid the lid shut, then pulled it back a fraction to let air in, and finally placed it at the bottom of his wardrobe and shut the door. *Phew.*

Suddenly the back door slammed.

'Robbie, Robbie!' his dad was calling in a loud whisper.

'I'm up here dad.'

'Shh, stay there.'

'But Dad.'

'It's Mrs Winterbottom from *de* Co-op.'

Robbie had never seen his dad in such a panic as he bounded up the stairs panting from his exertion.

Geoffrey had never shown any interest in women since Maureen had walked out, even after five years. Though Robbie was ok, he still missed her and still wanted to know why she had just *upped sticks* and gone. He still got money on his birthday and Christmas, but neither he nor his dad had any idea where she was.

Mrs Winterbottom, however, was definitely 'available'. She'd been the manageress at the co-op for as long as Robbie could remember, but only recently had been taking an interest in him or rather, his dad.

'If she comes to the door don't answer it,' ordered Geoffrey, 'Pretend we're not in.'

Within seconds the bell rang.

'SHH.'

Geoffrey was cowering in his bedroom, Robbie in his.

'Coo-ee, Mr. Harraby!'

The bell rang again. Robbie sneaked out to the top of the stairs and could see this large bright red figure through the frosted glass. Again, the bell rang insistently.

'Cooee! Mr. Harraby, I have some puddings you might like. All reduced, shame to let them go to waste. And I've saved a small bag of porridge for you, you know there's a shortage of it at the moment?'

Geoffrey wagged his finger and scowled at Robbie menacingly. The bell rang again and again. Then he heard a large sigh and steel-edged stilettos fading down the path.

'Has she gone?'

'I think so.'

'At last,' gasped Geoffrey. 'That was a close one! Right, I'm going for a lie down. Whatever you do, don't answer the door.'

''K dad. I might pop out later though.'

'Ok then, but be in for your tea, won't you?'

'Yes dad.'

Robbie waited a few moments, then when all was quiet, he opened the wardrobe door. To his horror the chess box lid was fully open and his sock halfway out. Sugar! Robbie thought and began ratching about in the piles of clothes resting at the wardrobe bottom.

'Looking for something, young man,' gasped a voice from his desk and turning round there was the mouse – slumped on his phone charger, with his arms flopped at his sides.

'Peter,' he panted, 'Guardian Peter, from Corliol.'

'I know,' replied Robbie, then corrected himself, 'well I didn't know your name.'

'But you guessed I was from Corliol?'

'Yes.'

'Then you know Jan.'

'Yes.'

'How did...?'

Peter waved his hand and closed his eyes.

'You look very tired.'

'Yes, I suppose I am,' sighed Peter, 'had a bit of a run-in with the felines. We have to work quickly, there's something very wrong.'

Not again, thought Robbie.

'In the meantime, you... erm... erm, you haven't any... biscuits, have you? Peter chomped, custard creams by any chance?'

Robbie dashed downstairs, and a minute later, handed Peter a piece of disappointing digestive, but Peter was obviously struggling to eat.

'I'm sorry,' he said, 'I'm just so tired. Something is wrong, very wrong,' he repeated, as he dozed off again. 'I'm so sorry, so sorry,' he muttered as he fell into a deep sleep. Robbie was about to leave him to rest when in the fogginess of unconsciousness, Peter seemed to be having a nightmare. 'No, no, no!' he called out. Robbie decided to wake him up, and slowly Peter sat bolt upright.

'We've got to do something!' he screamed.

'Calm down, calm down,' said Robbie, 'it's just a dream!'

'No, no, you don't understand. I'm so, so sorry, it's all my fault. It's real, it's real, it's going to happen tonight.'

'What is?'

'They're going to… going to…,' Peter froze in horror, 'They're going to steal a star!'

'Who is?'

'Satan, Luci, the felines!'

'Oh.' Robbie swallowed anxiously, remembering what Jan had said, how the felines wanted to start their own exchange. Peter placed his paw on Robbie's hand and looked him straight in the eyes.

'We've got to stop them, Robbie. The felines are going to steal the star tonight and… and it's all my fault… I told them how to do it.'

Robbie fell silent. *What on earth would you do that for*? thought Robbie. But Peter didn't answer, he just sobbed loudly, placing his head in his hands with tears running down his snout and body. *I hope my charger's going to be ok* worried Robbie.

'Look, don't worry,' Robbie comforted. 'I think Jan knows something's going down, and she's getting something ready. She said I should meet her there tonight.'

Peter came round, 'Really? Then there's hope. What time are you meeting her?'

'One a.m.'

'One a.m.? No! No! No!' Peter exploded, 'It will be too late. The raid's at midnight! We've got to get a message to her before it's too late.'

'Ok, but how?' queried Robbie, then had an idea. 'I could take one?'

'Yes, please. No, wait, there'll be no-one about till at least twelve-thirty when they start getting ready for prayers, and no-one will be able to use the portal till one a.m. What have I done? What have I done!' Peter repeated.

'And there's no way of opening the portal early?'

Peter shook his head tears re-forming in his eyes.

'Can we get to them while the cathedral is still open?' suggested Robbie, 'Maybe I could sneak in, and hide?'

'No good,' Peter replied. 'The verger does a thorough sweep before he locks up and all the doors are alarmed.'

'A note in the well or something?'

'I guess you could, but it will be well past midnight before Robinson starts opening up the portal: so by the time he finds it, it will all be over!'

The two fell silent in despair.

Then Robbie, more out of frustration than inventiveness said, 'Well, if the portals are going to be closed, and the doors alarmed, how are the cats planning to get in?'

Peter sat up.

'You're right, by golly. You're right. Somehow, they must have access to a key and the alarm code.'

'Vernon!' They said in unison.

Yes. Satan could steal it, anytime, Robbie thought.

'Our only hope then is to follow them in. But how? They are bound to see us.'

Peter held his paw in a fist, pressing it to his mouth as he thought. Then he sat bolt upright,

'Not if we go through a different door!'

'There's another door?'

'Uh-huh? That's it…we go in at exactly the same time they do.' Peter smiled. It was the first time Robbie had seen him anywhere near happy. Peter continued, 'As they go in the main door and silence the alarm.'

'Ok.'

'We'll go in the vestry door unseen.'

'Vestry door?'

This was news to Robbie.

'The vestry door is on the opposite side of the Temple. Now what do you Shallownessians call them?' He thought for a minute. 'Yes, yes, I know…a fire escape!'

'But wouldn't we need a key for that just the same?'

'Vernon will have one. All you need to do is get it from him.'

'*All?*' questioned Robbie.

'From the Verger's lodge of course!' added Peter, agreeing with himself.

CHAPTER 12 — MISSING IMPOSSIBLE

Satan and Luci reached the factory together. As they strode down the cellar steps, they knew something wasn't right. Satan turned to Luci placing his finger on his lips, then to his ear, listening.

'I don't hear anything,' Luci whispered.

'Precisely!' spat Satan, 'It's mid-morning, where are they all?'

Luci climbed up to the entrance of their lair, the old boiler room window, and peered in.

'They're all asleep!' she revealed, shocked.

Satan's eyes shifted from puzzlement to fear, and he turned, vaulted to the jammed office door and squeezed through it. Seconds later came a vocal explosion.

'Luci! Luci!' He erupted, 'He's gone! The mouse has GONE!'

Luci rushed over, slipped through and joined Satan who was staring at an empty cage.

'Impossible!' Luci screamed, filling her lungs in anger, 'I CHECKED the lock myself!'

'And where are Burke and Hare, the guards?' Satan continued.

Suddenly, they heard some whining behind them. Satan signalled with his head for Luci to take a look. She crept up to the door and extending her neck, snooped around it.

'You'd better come and see this,' she advised.

Satan sauntered behind her, placed his paws on her shoulders then raised his neck in shock. His whole pride was emerging from its lair so slowly and unsteadily, they looked like they had just dismounted from a waltzer. He took a deep breath through his nostrils, pushed her out of the way, and strutted into the cellar like a furious general about to berate his troops – his eyes flaming in anger.

'What's been going on?' He bawled, 'WHERE IS THE MOUSE?!'

The cats shuffled uncomfortably, wobbling uncontrollably, many holding their heads in their paws.

'Burke! Hare! Where is the mouse?'

Two smaller cats with heads bowed and ears uniquely folded frontways, staggered forward. They were the pride's night watch, and one of the few cats who didn't mind the graveyard shift.

'Forgive us master,' Burke pleaded, in his gentle *Edonburgh* accent, 'we only left him for a moment to join the others.'

'Then, all's blank,' Hare explained.

Luci squeezed through the window, and reappeared with the remainder of the pride and several empty plastic bowls. She laid them before Satan and pointed to the labels.

'Full-Cream-Sherry-Trifle?' He read, 'Reduced, for quick sale.'

Satan swept his burning eyes like a laser along the row of feline faces brave or stupid enough to return his gaze.

'We, we… found them piled up against the door,' M.C. grovelled, moulding his cap in his hands as he stared at the floor.

'You fools!' Satan scolded, 'Did none of you suspect it was a trick?'

Luci moved to Satan's shoulder. 'The work of a Shallownessian,' she whispered in seething rage; not just because Peter had escaped, but because she had lost her sumptuous treat (as everyone knew; *sacrimice* tasted much better than *mundomice*).

'I want him found,' Satan ordered. 'This puny mouse won't get the better of ME.'

'He can't be far,' agreed Luci.

Satan turned to the rabble before him. 'All of you, out! Out NOW! Yak, Uza, MC, Hunter, seal off the Cathedral – no mouse gets in or out! The rest of you – search the loading yard – bring me his bones if not his body!'

The pride began to mount the cellar steps: many still staggering, falling backwards, or walking into the walls.

Only three kittens remained in the boiler room, each wore a blue turban (to denote their military status) and each sat on a bag of oats, in the lotus position, deep in meditation – apparently unaware of what had been happening through the night.

Satan smiled.

'Shall I wake them?' offered Luci.

'No. no,' assured Satan, 'Let them rest, they deserve it. They were the only ones to keep themselves sober, and I need them to be rested to shell accurately tonight.'

(Sun, Dar and Singh, though the size of kittens, were actually fully grown rusty-spot cats from India; renowned mercenaries, who worked devastating catapults made out of large wooden shovels on pivots.)

Satan paced up and down, pounding one paw with the fist of his other. 'He'd better not have warned them!' he fumed.

'We'll get him, my King,' Luci calmed, taking his paws in hers and bending to kiss them. 'I shall do another search of the city centre then go home to make preparations for the battle.'

Satan kissed hers and, rather out of character, spoke quite tenderly, 'I don't know what I'd do without you, my Queen.'

(Little did he know that Luci's idea of *preparing*, involved a manicure, a visit to the Coiffure, and an afternoon at the spa with her friends from the book club.)

They mounted the steps together, hand in hand, and kissed as they went their separate ways.

CHAPTER 13 — THE STAKE OUT AND CLEAN OUT

Robbie gently placed the sleeping Peter back in the chess box and slid the lid across quietly.

He then crept downstairs, missing the dodgy steps. He could hear his dad's snores and sniffles as he pulled the back door shut and sped down the road. A stooped figure, in a large grey overcoat chomping on a profusely billowing pipe, greeted him.

'Hello Geoffrey!'

'It's me, Robbie,' he replied.

'Course it is,' replied Mr. Armstrong, squinting through the glacier-thick lenses of his dark square spectacles (in the process of pushing a torn plastic bag into the post box).

'No! Mister Armstrong!' Robbie shouted. But it was too late.

'What?' the old man queried, 'Got to recycle you know.'

'Never mind,' dismissed Robbie, but then froze, horrified, as Mr. Armstrong wandered up his neighbour's path, lifted up a lid, and placed a large bag of rubbish in their metal compost bin.

'Oh Mr. Armstrong!' called Robbie, 'Let me help you!' and gently he led him back down the path and into his own garden, retrieving the rubbish as he went.

'What?' Bernard asked, mystified.

'Nothing,' lied Robbie, exasperated, placing the rubbish in the proper wheelie bin.

'Just off to do the shopping!' Mr. Armstrong announced in a cloud of his favourite tobacco (Virginian Wolf), heading straight for his bright yellow Ford Capri, parked opposite. 'Want a lift into town?'

'No fear, I mean, thanks,' replied Robbie petrified.

He'd only been in Mr. Armstrong's car once, and it hadn't ended well. Mr. Armstrong's eyesight was so bad, he'd turned into someone's drive three times before getting the proper road.

'Catch you later,' Robbie sang, relieved.

Mr. Armstrong waved, then bent over, squinting for the keyhole in the door. No one in the street understood how he had kept his licence, but for some reason he had. (Many of the neighbours had woken up to find his car leaning against theirs – because on such a steep road he had forgotten to put the handbrake on.) His other love was of course music; and he used to drive down to the cathedral every evening to hear the Shallownessians sing evening prayers.

Robbie jogged down the Scaur, past the park and up towards the cathedral. *That's funny,* he thought, as he saw a large brown cat stretched out on the low wall at the corner of the cathedral gardens, then another like a sentry, at the castle gate entrance.

He crossed to the opposite side of the street and pulled down his army baseball cap. The cat didn't seem to notice him, it just stared at the pavement.

As Robbie approached the verger's lodge, another large cat was patrolling the wall there, scanning the gutters. They're obviously not looking for me, thought Robbie *phew*.

Robbie straightened up and nonchalantly took up his position on the wall opposite Vernon's front door. *I wonder where he keeps his keys?*

No sooner had the thought occurred than the burly figure of the neckless Verger appeared, picked up a bunch of keys from a hook on the wall, and stepped out into the bright sunshine.

If only I could get that ring, thought Robbie. He followed the waddling *gadgee* through the gates to the main door: but the keys looked firmly fixed to a clasp on his belt.

#

Geoffrey woke in alarm, his phone buzzing loudly.

'Hallo?' he yawned.

'Geoff it's Al Close, duty manager.'

'Oh, hello Mr. Close.'

'I know it's your day off, but we could really do with some help down here at the factory, we seem to have been invaded by cats and could do with some extra hands to get rid of them.'

Geoffrey held his silence.

'Obviously,' coughed Mr. Close, 'we'll pay you overtime.'

'Overtime? Sure,' said Geoffrey, 'I'll be *d'ere* as soon as I can.'

Geoffrey slipped his bike out of the shed and sped down the hill, across the bridge and reached the factory in less than ten minutes. Sure enough, the place was still crawling (quite literally), with disoriented cats.

Ian the other maintenance man, and Jenny the cleaner, were already swinging yard brushes at the hapless animals; but most were just staggering around in circles.

‘We knew we had a few in the cellars,’ said Ian, ‘but not this many!’

‘What’s up with them?’ asked Jenny, ‘anyone would think they were drunk!’

‘Too much sun if you ask me,’ tutted Ian.

‘*Dis* is useless!’ Geoffrey exclaimed. Then he had an idea. ‘Wait here a second.’

He raced next door to the furnishings shop, grabbed an abandoned trolley and dashed back to the loading yard.

‘Right, pick ‘em up and put them in here.’

Ian and Jenny got to work, and soon half the cats were stacked in the trolley, dozing happily.

‘I’ll be right back,’ assured Geoffrey, scooting towards the trolley park.

‘Is that you, Geoffrey?’ came a voice. A long grey coat appeared from a fog of tobacco.

‘Oh, *hullo*, Mr. Armstrong,’ Geoff flustered, as he casually shielded the laden trolley. Mr. Armstrong peered towards it.

‘You buying some rugs too? I’m getting some for the summer house.’

‘Er, yes,’ hesitated Geoff, nudging the trolley between two cars with his foot.

‘Apparently *d’ere’s* a shortage,’ he lied, adding, ‘*d’ere’s* a rush on.’

‘A rush? Good heavens, I’d better be quick!’ responded Bernard. ‘Toodle-pip,’ he waved, ‘a rush by Jove!’ and turned towards the shop in a cloud of Virginian.

Geoffrey felt a little guilty about lying to Mr. Armstrong, as he did tend to be a little gullible, but he really didn’t have the time to explain.

Mr. Close was in the yard when Geoff got back.

‘Excellent work, everyone!’ he praised.

Most of the remaining cats had been gathered by Ian and Jenny and with Geoffrey’s help they soon had them all piled in the new trolley.

‘Splendid idea,’ congratulated Mr. Close, ‘Where are you taking them?’

‘To the…’

‘Police, Vet, Park,’ Ian, Jenny and Geoffrey replied within milli-seconds of each other.

‘Sorry?’

Geoffrey leapt in, ‘To the park, Mr. Close.’

‘Very good,’ came the reply, as he headed back to his office.

Geoffrey exhaled deeply, winked at his co-conspirators, and wheeled the trolley back towards the car park.

CHAPTER 14 — TWO IMPERTINENT RAIDS

YAN:

After an hour or so, with no sign of Vernon appearing, Robbie retraced his steps from the verger's lodge and crossed to the other side of the cathedral.

Sure enough, there was the door Peter had spoken about, with *Fire Exit Keep Clear* emblazoned across it.

Glancing around to see if anyone was looking, he approached it. *Hmmm,* he thought, *definitely a keyhole, but it's bound to be alarmed too!*

Suddenly a shrill hooter sounded, and Robbie, jumped back in panic, *Oh no*, *they've seen me!*

He backed away, then realised that THAT looked equally suspicious; so, he turned sideways (as if he was simply walking past). Fixing his head down, pretending to study the grass: he strode out, half-walking, half-running to the pavement. *I'm for it now*, he sweated.

But as he finally plucked up courage to look up, he realised no-one was looking his way: all were staring across the road, where the alarm was sounding and people were pouring out of the Building Society.

'I bet it's only a test,' he heard a gadgee say, 'there's no smoke.'

Relieved, Robbie crossed over to get a better look. There weren't just members of the public pouring out the main entrance, but others, presumably staff, appearing from a second door around the corner.

It was then he saw them: three ginger toms sneaking into the staff entrance! The first was carrying a small step ladder, the others had rucksacks strapped to their backs.

Foily keaties! thought Robbie.

He kept watch, and a few moments later, the cats re-emerged, with much heavier bags. Robbie chased them.

'Oi. What do you think you are doing?'

The one with the step ladder, turned, arched his spine and hissed at him so violently that Robbie backed off. They then darted into a car park, turned a corner and disappeared.

Moments later, a fire tender arrived, and before long, everyone was ushered back into the building.

Robbie returned to sit on the wall opposite Vernon's lodge, and was becoming dispirited: *without the key. the whole plan would fail!*

And then it dawned on him. He smiled, leapt to his feet and hurried all the way home.

#

TYAN:

Around five o'clock, Robbie and Geoff were finishing off a local delicacy from the chip shop: home-made steak pie, chips, gravy and mushy peas. Geoff was recounting the escapade of the drugged cats, and how he'd met Mr. Armstrong in the car park in a cloud of smoke.

Suddenly they heard a car door slam.

'It's just Bernard off *to evendong*,' Geoff announced, nonchalantly.

'Hmm,' said Robbie thoughtfully; then suddenly sprung up from the table. *I wonder if he'll give me a lift*? Then added, 'Dad, I need to nip back to town for something.'

'What?'

'Just something.'

Geoff's face beamed. It was his birthday in a couple of days, and he was well-chuffed that Robbie had remembered.

'Go on then, but don't be long, it'll be dark *d'oon.*'

'Sure.'

Robbie grabbed his coat and managed to run down the road just as Mr. Armstrong was about to pull away.

'Mr. Armstrong! Mr. Armstrong!'

'Hmmm, yes?'

'You couldn't give me a lift into town, could you?'

'I suppose so,' he replied, 'but I'm only going to the cathedral.'

'That'll be fine.' Robbie grinned, and scuttled round to the passenger door and jumped in. He couldn't help noticing the back seats full of toilet rolls: but felt it better not to ask.

'Seat belt fastened?' squinted Mr. Armstrong.

'Yep,' replied Robbie, crossing his fingers in fear.

Mr. Armstrong released the handbrake and with a jerk, the car leapt forward. He didn't drive fast, just erratically, straining to see the curb and the lines in the middle of the road.

Robbie held on to his seat in horror as the Capri veered from lane to lane and vehicles pipped and honked from left and right. Robbie began to put his plan into action.

'Interesting news today, wasn't it?' Robbie engaged, plucking up the courage to risk distracting him further.

'What's that then?' Mr. Armstrong enquired, 'Can't really see the news anymore, my T.V.'s bust; it's gone all blurry.'

'About smoking being allowed back in public buildings.' Robbie grinned.

'Really? 'Bout time!' nodded Mr. Armstrong, swerving round a roundabout and narrowly missing a bus.

'And…,' Robbie froze for a couple of seconds as he thought he saw something moving in the gutter, something moving pretty fast. Robbie looked again but whatever it was had gone, or was never there.

'Nothing wrong with good baccy,' Bernard continued, then broke out into a wheezing coughing fit, sounding like a perforated squeezebox.

'I suppose,' Robbie replied. Then crossing his fingers, and hating to tell lies, he screwed up his eyes, adding: 'It's even allowed in churches now.'

'Really?' cheered Mr. Armstrong, cutting up a taxi to a constant blast of its horn. 'Well, I suppose it's no worse than incense.'

By the time they reached the cathedral, Robbie was feeling confident to peep out of one eye again, and Mr. Armstrong (whose face was glued to the windscreen, squinting) had slowed to a snail's pace, much to the annoyance of the drivers behind him.

'Here! Turn here!' instructed Robbie.

'Hmmm, where?'

'There! Where the gap is!'

'Yes, I know,' reposted the driver, as he pulled up into a car park oblivious he was parking at an angle across two spaces.

Robbie couldn't wait to get out.

'Thanks Mr. Armstrong, enjoy evensong and maybe…' Robbie bit his tongue, 'a smoke?'

Mr. Armstrong felt his way out of the car and shuffled up the street.

He reached the cathedral gates, quite unaware he was being watched.

'Evensong and a smoke,' he ruminated, 'Hmmm.'

He reached the main doors.

''Evening Mr. Armstrong,' welcomed Vernon, handing him a book.

''Evening, erm, evening erm...,' muttered Bernard, peering at the neckless wonder who was silhouetted against the low sun.

'...Vernon,' the verger emphasised.

'Oh yes, oh yes,' Bernard agreed ostensibly, but in reality, was still uncertain.

No sooner had Bernard sat down than the bell chimed three times and two columns of Shallownessian girls followed by two columns of adults, all dressed in ruby red and white vestments, moved down the central aisle and into the choir stalls. Vernon appeared at the back, leading the Dean and two canons.

'O Lord open thou our lips,' intoned the Dean, and the Shallownessian choir replied: 'And with thy spirit.'

Virginian Wolf, remembered Mr. Armstrong, patting his pockets in search of his pipe.

Vernon closed the archway gates and left for his vestry.

'Ahh,' triumphed Bernard as he pulled his pipe from his right-side pocket and his *baccy* from his left.

One of the choirgirls noticed him, her eyes popping out of her head as he proceeded to press the foul weed into the pipe bowl. She dug her elbow into the girl beside her when he pulled out his matches, struck the box several times, and then sucked in; the flame liberating a choking whiff of tobacco.

'Let our prayer rise before you as incense,' sang the choir – but not for long, because they were suddenly interrupted by a shrill siren and a flustered Vernon sweeping swiftly through the organ arch.

'Everybody out! Everybody out!' he called.

The organ played on as the choir stopped dead and the adults shepherded the choristers towards the main door.

Some visitors came up from the crypt and Vernon ushered them to his vestry. 'This way, nice and slow. Follow me please,' he instructed. He led them through to an outside door, smashed the glass on the emergency key holder, then placing it in the door shooed them out.

He then headed back to the choir at the main entrance.

Robbie immediately met them on the grass calling, 'This way, this way,' and as the evacuees stepped out, he gestured to them to go round to the front.

Quick as a flash, he then stepped inside, twisted the key from the door, and walked calmly out. He was more excited than afraid. *It worked! It worked!* He said to himself. He checked left and right, then pulled the door shut, and locked it – secreting the key in his pocket.

Just then an array of blue flashing lights turned the corner and two large red fire tenders roared up the road, followed by a police car, with sirens blaring.

Robbie's lips were pursed together with pride. But as he turned to walk away, three cats appeared, blocking his path. *O-oh,* he thought. An enormous white keaty crept past him and sniffed the door, then turned to stare at him in silent interrogation.

Robbie tried to relax. *Did she see me steal the key?*

He began to hum Jan's song, and his heartbeat and breathing calmed. The cat stalked nearer, raised its nostrils at him, and sniffed him up and down – like a security dog at an airport. Satisfied, it then turned to the other two, and flicked its head, signalling them to return to their posts.

Robbie huffed smugly. *Why not just tell them? I know you can all talk!* But as he made his way towards the main entrance, he realised that the cat, from a distance, was tailing him.

In the Cloister there was pandemonium: the choir were being ushered into the café, and registers were being called; various visitors were being gathered together and counted; and, *oh dear,* two police officers had hold of a bemused Mr. Armstrong!

Time to go, thought Robbie. But as he turned, he saw something in the gutter again, this time as clear as day.

CHAPTER 15 — ENTER THE WARRIORS

Though it lasted only a second or two, he was certain his eyes were not betraying him. There, like a passing mirage, was a line of six or seven sacrimice, wheeling the tiniest seven-seater motorbike you could imagine. They weren't dressed at all like guardians, THESE mice wore black leather jackets, faded jeans and biker helmets! Each was veiled in a kind of sniper netting – covered not in leaves but tiny mirror-glass and sequins. In sunlight, the effect was dazzling, as blinding as a flickering strobe.

Robbie learnt that, if he only glanced for a few seconds then immediately turned away, a decent image remained on his retina. He could make out that several of them were limping, the front of the bike was badly twisted, but the tricycle at the back looked fine.

Suddenly, something brushed against the back of his leg. *That damn cat!* he cursed.

Robbie took a deep breath then turned to face it. He kicked at it with his boot 'Shoo!' But the Cat raised its head defiantly. *If she gets past me, she's bound to find the mice*, he panicked.

Though they were difficult to see, he could now hear them chuntering quite easily.

'Wait until we find 'im,' one was saying, 'bloomin' maniac, shouldn't be on the road.'

'Didn't get the reg number,' another added, 'but I'd recognise it anywhere, big yellow thing it was.'

Robbie gulped. They all sounded very angry. The cat began to tilt her head inquisitively.

Oh no, thought Robbie, *it can hear something.*

Just as the cat began to move forward to look behind him, Robbie burst out singing, dancing (which he never did), and blowing raspberries.

The cat stopped, sat up and lifted an eyebrow in puzzlement (as did several people passing).

'Shoo!' Robbie repeated.

As the cat finally turned away, Robbie felt very proud of himself; until he, in turn, saw a whole crowd gathered speechless on the pavement, and right at the front: Mrs. Truelove, Catherine, and her dad, each with mouths stuck open, frozen in shock.

Robbie's mouth froze too, then stretched into a fake smile; but Mrs Truelove just shook her head slowly.

Catherine was trying not to laugh, but acted equally stern as her mam grabbed her hand and marched her away.

Robbie was now sure he needed to go home.

CHAPTER 16 — FINAL PREPARATIONS

Jan scampered up the steps of the Dean's Tower where she found the Prior on the window ledge, peering at the cathedral.

'False alarm,' he said calmly, 'where there's no smoke, there's no fire.'

'Well, they're here,' Jan reported.

'Can I take that back?' Marcus joked.

'They're in pretty bad shape though – an accident I believe.'

No sooner had she finished speaking than seven weary mice waddled into the room.

The Prior stood. 'Gentlemen!'

'And lady!' came a deep voice at the back.

'Sorry, lady?' the Prior replied, failing to hide his surprise at the heavily tattooed figure at the back with bulging biceps. Marcus cleared his throat. 'Thank you for coming. I trust you will find your accommodation satisfactory?'

'We'd better!' threatened the voice from the back.

'We'll manage!' fumed Hannibal – the leader of their chapter, annoyed that someone had spoken before him.

He'd been elected as their chaplain, not simply because of his long military service – but because of his strength and ferocity. He stood with a slight stoop, denim waistcoat, oil-stained jeans and fingerless gloves. But the most striking part of him was his face – or rather lack of it. Below a dark red helmet, capping the whole of his snout to just above his mouth, was a white skull-shaped mask. No-one was sure what he was hiding – only that it must be something horrific for him never to remove it when anyone was about.

Many described him as someone you wouldn't like to meet on a dark night; others though disagreed and argued you wouldn't want to meet Hannibal in broad daylight! Sadly, he ruled by fear not devotion.

'Payment,' he demanded in his customary gruff voice.

'Full food and board while you are here,' announced the Prior, 'and three sacks of cheese per month for four months afterwards.'

'Four,' countered Hannibal.

'Four months or four sacks?' enquired Marcus.

Hannibal looked puzzled. Marcus took pity on him.

'Four sacks for three months then,' concluded Marcus.

'Yeah,' agreed Hannibal, victoriously. '*Tha's* better.'

Jan and Marcus smiled at each other, Hannibal may be pretty tough but when it came to brains, he'd obviously been at the back of the queue.

'I'll let you settle in then,' Marcus suggested, 'and I'll ask Guardian Nathanael, our infirmarian, to pop round and help with some of your,' he paused, 'battle scars.'

With that, Hannibal grunted, and the Knights of Lonercost dragged their way down the stairs and back out the emergency pane – followed closely by Jan, who securely bolted it after them.

#

Beneath the factory floor Satan was not happy. It had been hours since he'd sent his main force to hunt for Peter, and only half had returned.

'And you haven't seen any of the others?' he quizzed.

They all shook their heads, no one brave enough to admit they had woken up in a shopping trolley round the corner.

'Let's go through the plan one more time,' insisted Satan. 'I don't want any mistakes.'

The pride gathered round. Satan rolled out the detailed plan of the Cathedral grounds across the table.

'At twenty-three hundred hours we assemble in the yard and check equipment.'

All assented.

'Ginger tom team, make sure you have your jemmies ready to turn the door handle.'

The ginger toms glanced at each other in agreement.

'M.C. and Hunter, you supply the force to drive the door open.'

M.C. gave a *thumbs up* to Hunter, who aggressively dismissed him with a flick of the head.

'Dragon Li Team, check you have a pencil for the alarm pad, and have one last rehearsal at forming the tower.'

Ho Lee, still nursing a nasty bite from the gargoyles, dutifully bowed with the others – a long-practiced, perfect synchronization.

'Artillery?'

The three rusty-spotted *kittens* touched their turbans in salute.

'Ready and waiting, Sahib'

'Yak and Uza, make sure you have the bowl, mirror and lid.'

(Both jerked their heads in unison.)

'The rest, make sure you have sharpened your claws, just in case of any trouble. At twenty-three fifty-five,' he continued, ‘when all the Shallownessians are in bed, and before the guardians have risen, we meet at the cathedral doors, where I’ll have the key. Is that clear?’ concluded Satan.

All nodded.

CHAPTER 17 — UNWELCOME VISITORS

Peter awoke in the chess box. He wasn't sure how long he'd been asleep or what time it was. He slid back the lid and crawled out. It was getting dark. The execution of his rescue started to come back to him. He had dreamt he was being lifted, then sure enough he'd awoken to find a Shallownessian picking him out of the cage, slipping him into a sock and tying it at the top.

He could hear the felines snoring and purring, so had decided not to bite his way out, wherever he was going would be safer than that cage! He did however gnaw a tiny hole in the sock so he could peep out.

He was carried up the steps, out of the cellar, across the loading yard, but then he'd lost all sense of direction as he was gently placed into a coat pocket.

A vehicle had pulled up and the Shallownessian had said something to the driver – he couldn't quite hear because the car radio was on loud – but he was pretty sure his rescuer was a woman.

A short journey later, she got out, thanked the driver, and stood for a moment, until the car had pulled away. He couldn't remember much else, as he'd fallen asleep again; but regained consciousness as he was being gently lifted and emptied onto some grass.

Though he couldn't smell any felines he was still wary, so lay motionless for some time, playing dead. He could sense the Shallownessian watching. Eventually he heard her footsteps moving away; and by the time he plucked up courage to poke his head out, she had gone.

Quickly he crawled into a hedge and waited for dawn.

He must have slept deeply, because he only came around at the crash and boom of cans being dropped into a plastic storage chest. He quickly made his move, tracing the sound to the back of the house, where a Shallownessian boy was emptying something in a bin. As the boy turned to go back inside, he had followed and slipped in behind him.

When the boy went to the fridge, he had scurried up the nearest cupboard and finally found a place safe enough to sleep.

Suddenly, Peter snapped out of his daydream, as in the darkness, one of the stairs creaked loudly, then another.

'Robbie? Robbie? Is that you?' came a man's voice.

He dived back into the wardrobe, jumped into the chess box and closed the lid; but not before knocking over a drinking glass of Robbie's favourite marbles.

Geoff appeared at the door, turned on the light, and grunted. Then he sighed as he saw the marbles scattered across the rug. He then noticed the chess pieces piled on the bed. *I don't know*, he said to himself. He knelt down, gathered the marbles first, and standing up the glass poured them back in.

He then went back to the bed, gathered the chess pieces and looked around for the box. After searching high and low, he peered into the bottom of the wardrobe. 'There it is,' he triumphed, as he caught sight of it under the shoe shelf.

However, as he went to pull it out, a black-coated mouse sprang from it and scampered up his sleeve. 'Argh,' jumped Geoffrey, and stood with hands raised like he was being arrested. Then he felt something moving in his jumper, but before he could respond, that beautiful chant caressed his ears again, and he fell to his knees, curling up like a little puppy into a deep sleep.

Peter waited a moment then scrambled out. 'Very good!' he chirped and, concluding he was in no danger, swiftly moved his attention to what might be in the kitchen, especially of the custard cream variety.

Robbie made it back home, just as the sun had set.

'Dad? Dad?' he called, as he switched the kitchen light on, 'What's for supper?'

But there was no answer. Then Peter suddenly appeared on the table. 'Ah, Master Robbie.'

'Peter. Where's Dad?'

'Ah.'

'Ah what?'

'He's sleeping.'

'What again? In bed?'

'Not exactly… er… in yours.'

'Why would…,' Robbie stopped, 'what's happened THIS time?'

'Don't worry,' Peter 'fessed, 'he's fine, and won't remember anything.'

Robbie stumbled up the stairs with Peter closely following, and found him snoring on his bedroom floor.

'And you're sure he won't remember?'

'Not a thing,' Peter assured. He then changed the subject. 'Well, how did you get on?'

Robbie triumphantly produced the key to the fire escape and waved it in front of him.

'Excellent, excellent,' Peter responded, clapping his paws. 'So, you got into his lodge you clever boy.'

'Didn't need to!' boasted Robbie, but before he could continue, Peter finished his sentence.

'Setting off the fire alarms, ingenious!'

'What, you heard them from here?'

'Oh Robbie,' Peter enthused, 'don't you see what this means? We can do it, we can save the stars!'

'We haven't done it yet,' cautioned the young lad, 'we still haven't worked out how to get a message to Jan. Oh, and there's some other mice hanging around who look a bit dodgy, came on a seven-seater motorbike.'

'Oh no,' Peter sighed, 'were they in leather? Led by a guardian with a red helmet?'

'Yes, how…?'

'The Knights of Lonercost,' Peter moaned, 'devastating against felines but devastating against everything! Last time, they fought off a pretty heavy onslaught of felines, successfully trapping them in the gates, but jammed the whole mechanics in the process, and it took Molly our engineer, months to sort – not to mention what they did to the grounds with their dynamice. I'm sure they're not allowed to use it officially.'

'Dynamice?'

'Oh, you'll see soon enough.' Peter exhaled. 'Don't worry, doesn't hurt Shallownessians, but the felines hate it. You did well to see the knights, their jackets are normally festooned with sparklers.'

'Sparklers?'

'Sort of mirror netting, it makes them almost invisible in daylight.'

Just then the doorbell rang, and a shrill voice erupted.

'Geoffrey! Geoffrey! I know you are in there!'

'On no, Mrs Winterbottom!'

'I have some *Fever Nurse* for your flu. You must look after yourself, you know. And I've brought you a lemon: you know there's a shortage at the moment! The vitamin C will do you good.'

The tall red figure shimmered through the frosted glass door.

'What do I do? What do I do?' panicked Robbie.

'Come on Geoffrey. I've brought my sweet Luci-wucy to say hello too!'

Robbie sneaked a peep from the landing. Mrs Winterbottom glanced up just before he could dive behind the curtain.

'I know you're in!' she shrieked. 'I've just seen you at the window! Now stop being silly and come and answer the door!'

'I'd better go,' he resolved, 'and you, Peter, better make yourself scarce, she's got her keaty with her.'

'Cat?' Peter flustered, and with that, he scrambled up onto Robbie's shoulder and peered onto the path.

'Great Tolfink!' He erupted, 'That isn't a CAT! that's Lucifer, Satan's second in command!' Peter automatically scampered behind Robbie's neck and cowered, screaming, 'Whatever you do, don't let her in!'

He then bolted along the carpet back into Robbie's bedroom and buried himself in the wardrobe.

The bell rang again, one constant ring.

'Coming, coming,' Robbie called, 'I'll just tell her he's not in,' he whispered, and switched on the light.

When he got to the door, he smoothed his jumper down, took a deep breath, and pulled it open.

‘Stop being so ridiculous,’ she chided, marching into the hallway before he had a chance to block her, ‘now where is your father?’

‘Out,’ Robbie replied.

‘Nonsense,’ she dismissed, ‘I haven’t seen him all afternoon, and if he goes out he always passes the shop.’

‘No, really,’ Robbie persuaded, ‘believe me, he really IS *out.*’

She was looking in the hall mirror, straightening her hat and checking her lipstick – no mean feat with a handbag over one arm, a package from the chemist and a large cat in the other.

Robbie smiled at the golden Persian, and stretched out to stroke it, as it seemed to be in some pain – its eyes watering. But it moved its head to avoid his touch, then turned it to one side, expressionless, staring into his eyes as if searching them. Robbie retreated to a safe distance.

‘Oh, don’t mind Luci,’ she laughed, ‘she’s very friendly, aren’t you kitten?’

‘Look I’m really sorry, but dad IS out,’ Robbie pressed.

‘Rubbish,’ she replied, calling his name as she searched the kitchen and lounge. ‘The poor thing must have gone to bed.’ And with that she began marching up the stairs. ‘Which is his bedroom?’

Robbie pushed past her and rushed to close his father’s bedroom door.

‘In there, hey?’ she commented, then knocked on the door, switched on the light, and barged in.

‘Now listen Geoff…’ but then she saw that, indeed, the double bed was empty. ‘Mm,’ she huffed. ‘Are you sure he’s not in?’

Seizing the initiative Luci wriggled free, sniffed the air and strode into the bedroom next door. 'I'll, I'll get her,' Robbie stammered cheerfully, but it was too late and Mrs. Winterbottom blundered into his bedroom after Luci, switching on the light.

'Goodness me!' she exclaimed, seeing the figure curled unconscious on the floor, 'Quick, call an ambulance!'

'Oh heck!' Robbie gasped in mock surprise, 'Dad! what are you doing in here?!'

'Out of the way,' she called, licking her lips, with a devilish smile, and adding eagerly, 'this calls for mouth-to-mouth reverberation,' and before he could stop her, she had dropped to her knees, jettisoned her bags, and lovingly took his dad's head in her hands. She gazed into Geoffrey's closed eyes adoringly for several seconds, sighed, then placed her ear to his mouth. Geoffrey sighed and smiled, giving her completely the wrong impression.

More worrying to Robbie though, was her Golden Persian, who, having sniffed around the bedroom, was now heading for the wardrobe, following a trail of biscuit crumbs.

'He's definitely breathing,' she assessed, with disappointment, kneeling up again.

'Here kitty, kitty,' Robbie called out.

But Luci froze, stared right back at him, looked at the wardrobe, looked back at Robbie, then bending low and licking her lips, crept into it.

Mrs Winterbottom gently lifted Geoff's head with one hand and placed the fingers of her other on his forehead. 'Dearie me,' she frowned, 'He's definitely running a temperature.'

Still focused on the cat, Robbie seized the opportunity, 'You don't think it's contagious, do you?'

Mrs Winterbottom dropped Geoffrey's head in a reflex action, his skull slamming into the parquet floor with a thud and a groan.

'I shouldn't think so.' She recovered, wiping her hands on her dress, then sitting back with embarrassment. 'But best be careful.'

'Honestly Mrs Winterbottom, he'll be fine,' and to reassure her he added, 'he does this a lot.'

'He does?'

Robbie's mind went blank. 'Er… ever since…'

'Ever since your mother left?'

Robbie had no option, 'Yes, yes, that must be it,' he agreed.

Mrs Winterbottom wiped a tear from her eye.

'Well, he is a good colour I guess, and he does seem to be breathing perfectly normally, if not snoring? Perhaps he'll be better after a good night's sleep.'

She then leant forward, ratched through her handbag, and pulling out a baby-wipe, began scrubbing her hands furiously.

Just then there was shriek from the wardrobe, and a black smudge shot across her face, followed by a flash of golden fur in pursuit.

'Arrgh!' she screamed, as she twisted her body away three hundred and sixty degrees, crashing onto the floor.

'Peter! Peter!' Robbie shouted, as he dashed along the landing after them. He could hear pots, pans and glasses exploding across the kitchen. He slid down the banister rails, landed in the doorway, and made a grab for Luci as she bounded across tables, worktops and shelves.

Then suddenly there was a *slam* and 'Me-ow!' from the fridge freezer, as Peter scrambled underneath it and Luci collided with the solid door.

'Naughty Cat!' Robbie shouted; but within a second Luci had regained her composure, turned angrily towards him, arched her back, and, hissing wildly, stretched out her talons.

Oh no, thought Robbie, *Steri-strips here we come.*

'Luci? Luci darling,' came a moan from upstairs, 'come to momma baby!'

Luci's eyes were both aflame and deadly cold at the same time.

'One day, Shallownessian,' she threatened, 'one day we'll be back. And there'll be no adult to save you then.'

Robbie gulped and backed away behind the table. Then mercifully, Luci turned towards the stairs, shook herself down, and tried to lick her coat back into its meticulous impeccability.

'Ahh,' she spat. 'I will have to make another appointment at the coiffure's now. You'll pay for this boy! In blood!' And before she disappeared, she turned her head back and hissed, 'Don't forget, we know where you live!'

Robbie daren't move, but glanced round the doorway to see Mrs Winterbottom limping down the stairs, gripping the banister with both hands, her dislodged hat covering one side of her face, and straggles of hair, the other.

'Lucy my angel. Momma needs to go home, momma isn't feeling well.'

The cat leapt up into her arms; and woman, cat, handbag and hat, made their way to the front door.

‘Tell your dad, I’ll be in touch later,’ Mrs Winterbottom slurred, as she went. ‘I think I lost conscientiousness.’

Robbie feigned a smile. ‘Thanks for coming,’ he added cheerfully, then rushed to shut and lock the door. He leant his back against it, catching his breath in relief.

CHAPTER 18 — ARMING, ATTACKING AND ESCAPING

Hannibal had ordered his chapter up early, at the very turn of dusk. 'Chapter parade now!' he shouted, as they tumbled out of their hammocks and shelters in the hedges, and formed a line in front of him, several still sporting bandages and bruises.

'I want everyone ready,' Hannibal grumbled, distractedly, as he passed along the line. 'It's already dark! Let's run through your duties. Gripper?'

'Yeah chaplain,' grunted the large muscle-bound Knight at the end.

'I want *the wheel* ready and loaded.'

'Yeah *chap*,' she replied.

He then pointed at two near the front, 'Scar and Pox you help.'

Both fist-bumped each other.

'Greaser!'

'Yeah *H*.'

'Damage report.'

Greaser scratched his head and turned towards their bike leant against the bushes.

'Front wheel knackered, rest ok.'

Hannibal scanned it slowly. The bike consisted of six ape-handled Harley Dovidsons, all linked together, with a final trike at the back, sporting solid panniers and a massive ghetto-blaster.

'We *gotta* uncouple,' advised Greaser.

'Do it,' agreed Hannibal.

'Bars?'

There was no answer.

'Bars!' Gripper elbowed him in the ribs.
'What?' He awoke.
'Where are we on the Dynamice?'
'Don't you worry about that *H*, done plenty.'
'Flower?'
'H?'
'You're on first watch…'
'Yes, H.'

And so it was that Gripper, Scar, Pox, Greaser, Bars and Flower limped into action. (Let the reader understand, there was nothing *floral* about Flower. Born in America he'd been a successful prize-fighter in the rodent Olympics but had given it all up to join the Knights. They'd only nicknamed him 'flower' after his cauliflower ears: which seemed to complement his broken snout and permanent fat lip.)

'Just give me sight of those felines,' muttered Hannibal, looking into his bike mirror as he fitted his helmet and straightened his mask.

#

Back in the boiler room the cats were busy preparing. Suddenly Luci appeared in the doorway. 'We must go NOW,' she called. 'I've found the rodent!'

'Excellent,' replied Satan, 'Where is the fugitive?'

'He's lodging with a human the other side of the river.'

'Ok,' Satan pondered, looking around his depleted forces, 'M.C. and Hunter, pick up the platoon that's guarding the cathedral and take them to seal off the house. Just make sure you're at the cathedral by Twenty-three fifty.'

The two large felines looked at each other, nodded, then went to Luci for directions.

'And ask around again, we need to find out who is holding the rest of our troops. Right comrades, everyone else to your stations and be sure to brief our missing compatriots on their return. Luci and I will go to our respective humans, and then meet you just before midnight.' Then he added rather threateningly, 'Don't dare be late.'

#

Peter emerged from the back of the freezer, 'We need to move now!' he pressed.

'But it's only eight o'clock,' argued Robbie, and we won't be able to get in till after midnight.'

'But she knows where we are,' Peter stressed, pacing the kitchen window on look out, 'and it won't take her long to report to Satan, and what, twenty minutes before they get here?'

Robbie felt a chill down his spine as he pictured the return of Luci taking her revenge.

'We need somewhere to lay low for an hour or two.'

'Like where?'

'Anywhere, as long as it's nearer town – so they can't cut us off.'

Robbie wracked his brains, *the Co-Op?* – no, they *couldn't hang about there, they could be seen by any passing cat.*

'Don't you know anyone further down the road?' Peter pushed.

A light flashed across Robbie's face, then he grimaced and shook his head.

'Come on,' said Peter, 'you had someone then...'

'Well, there is Mr. Armstrong's,' Robbie muttered.

'How far?'

'Four doors down.'

'Does he have any pets?' Peter queried, 'Any cats?'

'Just chickens,' answered Robbie, 'out the back.'

'Right, let's get some things together and head there then, the bonus will be that we'll be able to see when they get here.'

Within minutes, Robbie had picked up his scope, phone and goggles and having checked the street, was making his way down the hill, Peter riding shotgun in his front pocket.

#

Soon, Robbie and Peter were at Mr. Armstrong's gate. The path to the door naturally flanked by red solar lamps. As usual, he could be seen in his favourite armchair, encased in headphones, conducting his orchestra.

'We can't just turn up,' Robbie hesitated, 'I never call on him.'

'What never?' queried Peter.

'Well, only when I have a lesson,' Robbie explained.

'Lesson?'

'Singing,' Robbie smiled proudly, 'Did you not see me on Corliol's Got Talent?'

'No,' Peter replied, bluntly. 'And you see him no other time?'

'Well, there is Christmas,' Robbie explained, 'we always take him some mince pies at Christmas.'

'That's it then,' Peter concluded. 'Job's done.'

'I suppose,' agreed Robbie, and manfully he opened the gate and strode up to the front door. There was no bell, so Robbie knocked quietly. Mr. Armstrong didn't move, or rather continued conducting, oblivious.

'Knock harder,' Peter instructed.

Again, no response.

'Tap on the window.'

Robbie felt awkward but leant across and tapped with his fingertips. Mr. Armstrong sat upright and looked towards the window, squinting. He placed his headphones on the table at the side of his armchair, pushed himself up and left the room. Peter ducked down into Robbie's pocket.

'Is he coming or what?'

'Ssh, he's getting something in the hallway.'

A few seconds later there was a rattle of a chain and the door opened. 'I'll need two pints of semi-skimmed this weekend,' he announced, 'and here's what I owe you up till today.'

'It's me, Mr. Armstrong, Robbie from up the road.'

'Robbie?'

'Geoffrey's son.'

'Geoffrey?'

'Oh, Geoffrey. Geoffrey from up the road? Ah yes, come on in.'

As they entered the hall Robbie had to thread himself through boxes of salt and vinegar crisps – no doubt because someone had said there'd be a shortage. Mr. Armstrong went back to his chair and beckoned Robbie to take the one opposite. Robbie slalomed through bundles of papers and carefully moved a pile of manuscripts off the chair.

'Geoffrey, yes, I see.' Mr. Armstrong continued.

'Well, it's Robbie actually,' Robbie corrected.

'Oh ROBBIE!' Mr. Armstrong triumphed, 'Why didn't you say so? I was beginning to wonder why you'd lost so much weight.'

'Weight?'

'Height!'

'Height?'

'Hmmm,' he rasped with a cough, 'what can I do for you?' Then he paused in concentration, 'Dear, dear, *hmm*… Robbie?'

'*Em*... just thought I'd call and… and... say hello?'

Suddenly there was a nip in his chest.

'Ouch.'

'Sorry?'

'And wondered how you liked the mince pies we gave you at Christmas?'

'Mince pies? Christmas?' Mr. Armstrong looked puzzled.

'I know it was a while ago,' added Robbie.

'Was it?' came the reply. 'Well I never.'

'So, I'd just come to see how you found them?'

'Found them?' Mr. Armstrong thought seriously (wondering how he had lost them in the first place), and then concluded 'I see.' (Though obviously he didn't.)

Suddenly Robbie felt a wriggle under his shirt, then movement round the back of his collar. 'Keep still will *ye*?' he said, rather more loudly than he'd intended.

'Well, I'll try,' apologised Mr. Armstrong.

'No, not you,' Robbie sighed, making Mr. Armstrong search left and right for the other person he must be addressing.

'Get him to close the curtains,' whispered Peter, now tucked behind Robbie's ear.

'They DO say Mr. Armstrong…'

'They do?'

'Yes, they DO say, you… *erm…* save up to fifty percent of your light if you draw the curtains at night.'

'Really? Then I must do it immediately,' agreed Mr. Armstrong, muttering, 'it will stop the snails looking in anyway.' He raised himself from his chair, shuffled over to the window, but as he began to draw them, he paused for a second…staring. 'Well, I never,' he coughed again, 'Are those cats? Never seen so many!'

'Get down!' squeaked Peter, and Robbie dived between the papers.

When Mr. Armstrong turned round, he looked startled, peering at the empty chair. Then bemused, as he looked down, and saw Robbie, full length on the floor. Robbie's eyes moved from side to side in embarrassment, Mr. Armstrong's moved from side to side in puzzlement.

'The... the... money's all here you know,' offered Mr. Armstrong, 'You don't need to look for more.'

Robbie opened his mouth to speak, but no words came out. Instead, he got up, made a thing of dusting his knees and sat back in the chair. 'That should do it,' Robbie announced, bluffing.

'Do what?'

'Straighten the carpet!' Robbie replied authoritatively. 'They say a full length stretch every so often keeps your carpets straight.'

'They do?' said Mr. Armstrong keenly, 'Then you must come round more often and do it again.'

Robbie realised Peter was no longer behind his ear. He began patting his shirt and pockets. Mr. Armstrong stared at him.

'Lost your baccy Geoffrey? – Have some of mine!'

'No... no…,' Robbie couldn't think of anything worse. 'Just… just…'

Then he saw a lump moving along the curtain on the windowsill. Mr. Armstrong followed his gaze.

'Something the matter?'

'No, no,' replied Robbie, and turning his head, tried to distract him with, 'just thought how well the carpet looks now.'

'It does?' and as Mr. Armstrong stared at the floor Robbie looked back to the window, to see Peter's head appear around the middle of the curtains. He held up five fingers then did it again!

'Sugar!' exclaimed Robbie.

'I'm so sorry,' said Mr. Armstrong. 'Have I forgotten it again?'

'What?'

'You know. I don't even remember making the tea.'

'Oooh, tea, that would be nice,' capitalised Robbie.

'Certainly,' replied Mr. Armstrong, 'won't be a minute.'

With Mr. Armstrong out of the room Robbie shot to the window and peeped through the curtain.

'At least ten,' whispered Peter, 'they're surrounding your house – now's the time to move, while they're all occupied.'

#

Geoffrey again awoke surprisingly calm and carefree. He looked around and saw he was in Robbie's room. He could remember starting to tidy it up, but after that – nothing. The house was in darkness, lit only by the yellow streetlamps. 'Robbie? Robbie?' he called.

A curious sweet-smelling scent lingered in the air, but there was something much more pressing to investigate: poor Tutha, next door, was going wild. *Bill and Maggie must be out,* he decided, *I hope she's ok.* He strode to Robbie's window to find her not only running up and down the fencing like a maniac but barking uncontrollably. *Better go and see,* he resolved.

But when he switched on the landing light – nothing happened. *Bulb's gone – typical.* He glanced downstairs and was sure he saw something moving by the front door. He looked closer and could definitely make out the silhouette of a cat, that seemed to be holding its nose!

Geoffrey was amazed (they never got cats in the front garden because the people before them hated them, and so had planted loads of lemon balm and citrus trees, to keep them away). He would have thought nothing of it, but on reaching the bathroom, THAT light didn't work either, and another cat was perched on THAT window-ledge too.

No wonder Tutha's going mad, he laughed. *But why so many cats?* He turned his attention back to the lights. *I bet the fuse box has tripped,* he reasoned. He felt his way to his bedroom to get his phone, but on entering, he couldn't believe his eyes. There, three or four cats were *ratching* through his drawers and wardrobe, two of them wearing mining helmets!

When they saw him, they froze; but after checking him for weapons with their search beams, they simply went back to work!

'Oi!' Geoffrey challenged, 'What do you think you're doing? Shoo, Shoo,' he shouted.

But they hardly moved. Feeling brave, Geoffrey tore his duvet from the bed and advanced menacingly, swinging it around his head like a matador.

'Time for blood!' hissed Hunter, leaping on top of a wardrobe.

'We, we, betta scoot, and get to the Temple,' panicked M.C., rounding up the others and leading them out of the open window. Hunter remained motionless, staring down on his prey.

Geoffrey confidently crept closer, then suddenly, stopped. In the streetlamp haze he began to appreciate how big the cat actually was. It had a spotted coat and muscular body*, more of a leopard than a cat!* he thought – but it was too late. Without any warning, Hunter swooped down mercilessly, talons outstretched.

'Owwwwww,' Geoffrey screamed as it ripped into his scalp, and shouted, 'Get off me you daft cat!'

But before he could wrestle it to his bed, Hunter quickly gathered himself, smiled, and leapt through the window to join the others.

#

Robbie, with Peter on his shoulder, didn't delay. With Mr. Armstrong clattering in the kitchen, Robbie tiptoed into the hallway and slipped out the front door. He got down on his hands and knees and crawled to the gate. Peter skipped down and looked up the road.

'There's only one stationed on the pavement,' he whispered. 'And it's watching the house not the road. Keep your head down and cross over to the cars, they'll give us cover.'

Emboldened, Robbie dashed across and crouched between two parked cars. Peter scampered onto the bonnet of one, then up onto the roof.

'All clear!' he whispered, 'Good to go.'

He slipped into Robbie's pocket, who immediately began crawling down the hill.

It was then, it happened. Two rather familiar shoes came into view. He looked up to see Mrs Truelove, her arms folded, looking customarily stern.

'I, I can explain?' Robbie stuttered.

'That's it!' she concluded, 'I'm going to have a word with your father.'

'Please, please don't,' pleaded Robbie, 'he'll ground me for weeks. I'm not doing any harm, honest. You see I'm an astronomer, I only stay out at night to look at the stars.'

'Underneath cars?' she challenged.

Robbie took a deep breath but was defeated. Mrs Truelove walked on, shaking her head again.

'Quick,' said Peter, 'run for it!'

And keeping his head low, Robbie belted down the hill.

#

Robbie and Peter made good time. They hugged the cathedral wall past the fire exit and carefully peeked round the gates to monitor the main door. Sure enough, about ten or twelve felines were gathered there, with Satan and Luci.

'It's definitely tonight then,' whispered Peter, 'let's get back to the door.'

They had just reached their position, when they caught sight of a horde of cats running up the street.

'Down!' cried Peter, and Robbie went flat out into the grass.

The cats leapt the cathedral wall and cut through the trees passing the fire escape.

Robbie placed his hand over his mouth to hide his breathing. They herded on obliviously; until one of the largest, with a spotted coat, came to a halt, barely a metre in front of them. It began sniffing the air, intrigued by something nearby. It then began licking something from its paws – something that, in the floodlights, looked very much like blood!

Robbie's stomach churned. A bit of steak pie surfaced in his mouth with an acidy coating, and he knew he was going to be sick. Peter, hearing Robbie's retching, crawl-ed up to his face and placed his finger to his lips. Robbie could hold himself no longer. He pushed his face down deeper into the grass, screwed his eyes shut and began taking tiny rapid breaths, waiting for the talons to rake his head. *I can't do this*, he told himself, *I can't just lie here and let it rip me to pieces. This thing wasn't a cat, it really was a monster!* He'd had enough. He wanted to run and take his chances, but then, he knew, all would be lost if he did. Jan's words came back to him: *Are you a man or a mouse?*

But then he thought about the scars and Catherine. *She'll never look at me again! I'd RATHER be a mouse than a boy with a doubly scarred face!* he decided.

Suddenly, he saw himself in his infant classroom. A girl had pointed to his cheek, curled her lip, saying 'urgh'. He'd immediately buried his head in his arms and placed them on his desk, trying to hide the tears.

It was then he'd felt a hand on his arm, and looking up, saw Catherine's smiling face, leaning over, her head at an angle, like an inquisitive dog.

'That was unkind,' she judged. 'My mam says everyone has scars, just most are hidden – because they're on the inside. Look!' And she lifted up her arm showing him a dry, red patch above her elbow. 'A kettle,' she added in explanation.

(Her kindness was one of the reasons he really loved her, *no*, liked her, he corrected.)

Seeing he was unconvinced, she had then added: 'My mam says, 'True beauty is who you are on the inside, not how you look on the outside.''

He'd always treasured those words and they'd still brought him comfort whenever he looked in the mirror – except last week when he found an enormous zit on his nose.

Jan's words also came to mind: why the sacrimice had rated humans as *shallow*. The fact that Shallownessians' hearts were always focused on *lesser* things (like outward appearances and status, as they compared themselves to filtered selfies or sought control over others) rather than delighting in their true identity, as precious, unique, gifts of the Maker – stars in their own right.

'Very good, very good,' Peter suddenly interrupted, 'It's gone. We're safe.'

Robbie's mind stopped racing, but he couldn't help tracing the scars on his cheek with his fingers. *I guess they're not THAT big*, he consoled himself. *And if Catherine could put up with one set of scars she could put up with another?*

'Sure, sure, sure,' Peter broke in again, initially to Robbie's surprise. But then it turned to anger as he remembered that Peter too had, no doubt, been *listening in* all along.

They held their position, spying from a deep shadow in an alcove just outside the gates.

The cathedral clock struck the first chime of midnight.

'Here goes,' announced Peter, on the last gong of the clock, 'it's now or never.'

Which again shocked Robbie as it was exactly what HE was thinking.

CHAPTER 19 — INTO BATTLE

Outside the main doors Satan raised his arm. 'Right,' he ordered, 'begin the bombardment.'

The three Turban-clad *kittens* loaded their siege-engines and immediately catapulted large wodges of porridge high onto the tower, successfully immobilising three Scoobies.

Seconds later, the remaining two sentinels were hit, and similarly restrained. Next, the ginger tom team went to work, taking Satan's key, turning it in the lock and then expertly lifting the door handle. M.C. pushed forward and the Dragon Li team advanced inside, and forming their pyramid on each other's shoulders, tapped in the alarm code.

Suddenly a loud explosion erupted from the cathedral gates. Satan and the others scattered for cover.

'Yak, Uza,' Luci commanded, 'check it out.'

Robbie and Peter stepped back deeper into the shadows.

The Siamese bodyguards reached the gates in seconds: but Hunter was already there.

The large bin outside the gates had exploded and spewed out a pool of black, foaming liquid. Hunter sniffed it suspiciously. Yak and Uza prised the bin open, to find a tiny wooden crate packed with old, deformed plastic yoghurt bottles, some still leaking, others blown completely apart.

'We must tell Satan,' they decided.

'Nooooo!' Peter let out an elongated scream, so vehemently that Robbie had to smother him and pull him back deeper into the shadows. Robbie waited, then took a quick peep.

Hunter was looking around – thankfully more towards the shops and city centre than the cathedral. After a few sniffs, he went to join the others.

'What are you playing at?!' scolded Robbie.

'Sorry, sorry,' Peter excused, 'but that was a whole month's supply gone down the drain – literally!'

'Supply of what?'

Peter was too upset to speak, and just waved his hand signalling that it didn't matter.

'We need to get to the Fire Escape,' he insisted.

#

Robbie quickly hurried back along the wall and they both placed their ears to the door, concentrating. When they heard the beeping stop, and the alarm panel fall silent, they turned their key and hesitantly pushed it ajar – ready to run – but nothing sounded!

'It worked! It worked!' Peter whispered, jumping up and down.

Robbie was more anxious than excited. He slipped through the door, and closed it quietly behind him, then tiptoed past the sink and shelves to the inner door (sealed with a night latch). Robbie took a deep breath, turned the catch and delicately pulled the door towards them.

Opposite, were the high painted tableaus that formed the backs of the canons' stalls – perfect cover. Peter scurried up Robbie's leg and took a lookout position on his shoulder.

Robbie rushed forward, and placed his back to the paintings, checking left and right. They could hear the felines' chatter moving closer. Slowly and deliberately, as if he were moonwalking, Robbie crept to the end of the arches and peeped around.

The felines were now quietly but purposefully making their way towards the organ screen. Silhouetted against the open door, Satan was striding in behind them, with Yak and Uza following, carrying the dreaded bowl, mirror and lid.

'We've got to wake the Guardians!' cried Peter, and without thinking, in full view of the intruders, he slid down Robbie's coat and dashed towards the nearest brass lift.

He was but centimetres away when a ginger tom snatched him. Robbie gasped, clenching his fists, his mouth taut with stress.

Seeing Peter hanging upside down by his leg made Satan huff and smile. He raised his arm, and they all focused on the wriggling mouse.

'Welcome back,' he announced sarcastically, 'just in time for a snack.'

Robbie wanted to rush forward, he really did, but the fear of more scars persuaded him to stay hidden. *Oh Peter! – I just can't!* He felt helpless, but then caught sight of the old ship's bell which the canons and guardians used to signal the start of their services.

(It had come from the city's battleship, HMS Comberland, but was affectionately known as Ruby – after its distinguished captain – a DSM and expert in marine life.) Robbie sprinted up to it and asked permission to ring. 'Aye, Aye, *Cap'n.*' Ruby replied, and within seconds the bell was ringing furiously. 'Dang, dang, dang, dang…'

Luci dashed forward, 'It's the boy!' she shouted, 'Rip him to pieces!'

But before any of them could move, an incredibly loud roar sounded from the main door behind them. Twisting back, they all saw a cloud of dirty black smoke.

Satan looked at Luci, and she shrugged her shoulders equally clueless, but as the smoke began to dissipate, the roaring grew louder, and three small figures appeared from the fog, mounted on miniature motorbikes.

Satan froze. 'Leave the boy!' He screamed, looking perturbed, 'Get those knights!'

His forces turned quickly and charged towards them, talons outstretched. Peter was dropped unceremoniously as even the ginger toms joined the charge.

It's now or never thought Robbie.

Dashing forward, he threw himself towards the organ arch in a forward roll, scooping up Peter as he passed. Then he took cover behind a pillar in the chapel.

Within seconds the cats were twisting left and right trying to snatch Hannibal, Bars and Pox, zooming past them: in and out, behind and in front, each, it appeared, with a pillion passenger lobbing sticky lime bon bons.

'What is this stuff?' cried a Dragon Li, 'It smells vile.'

'It won't come off,' panicked another, 'what is it?'

Then one of the riders with a skull for a face, headed straight for them.

'Take this!' He called, 'Have some more dynamice!'

The felines swiped furiously at the mounted mice, but were so distracted by the need to pull out the sweets that were matting in their coats, they were quite unaware of a whole succession of guardians, emerging from the brass lifts behind them.

Marcus and Lesley were at the front, and led them through the organ screen, to the stalls, closely followed by Ben with a lime-loaded speargun and Sam on his skateboard with a sling, and a pouch crammed with grapefruit segments.

Indeed, all the guardians were carrying a range of weapons, from Shallownessian syringes (laced with fresh lemon juice), to aprons overflowing with Gustav's miniature lime tarts.

Harold brought up the rear, circling above them, and William was the rearguard, brandishing his trusty crossbow, each bolt with its own grapefruit warhead.

Satan retrieved Yak, Uza and Hunter and directed them towards the stalls. But as he led them through the arch, he was shocked by what stood before him. There, almost as tall as he, stood a pyramid of mice, topped by a rodent with spikey hair, back turned against him.

In one swift movement, each mouse loosened one arm, then placed something in each ear (apart from Ben and Sam, who each placed a thumb on their temples, stuck out their tongues, then waved their fingers at Satan, mouthing: *nur, nur, nur-nur nur*).

Satan exploded, 'How dare you!' He then took a deep, deep, breath and bellowed in fury, 'Annihilate them! Every one of them!'

But before any of the pride could move, a loud 'boom' erupted, followed by another, and a rhythm emerged.

'Duff-duff boom, duff-duff boom, duff-duff boom,' building louder, as each guardian joined the rhythm with hands or feet, Robbie and Peter saw Hikaru in the choir seats, his drum skin stretched across a stall with a Shallownessian microphone beside it.

Yak and Uza took a step back, believing it to be a Samurai call to war. Satan lifted his head in disdain.

But then the figure at the top with spiked hair turned around revealing she was holding an electric guitar. Suddenly the speakers erupted with a piercing scream, followed by a cascade of chords and riffs, as she and Bob (who appeared behind Hikaru), answered each other.

M.C. straightened up, impressed, and was just about to say so when he caught Satan's eye. Again, Satan drew in his breath to sound the charge, but then a deep bass single note (more like a foghorn than a voice), began bouncing from wall to wall. Maximus, radio mike round his neck, stepped forward.

The cats covered their ears in pain. So did Robbie and Peter. Then as the drum and screeching guitars and bass merged, the guardians all looked to Hamish the brass eagle, who began to rap!

The cats just froze in astonishment (all except M.C. who had closed his eyes, and was happily jerking his neck and shoulders to the music).

Hamish began to chant:

Satan you're a smell, givin' us hell,
taking all the grounds, thinkin' you'll be King someday,
you got lime in your fur, you stinking cur,
matted in knots like the sewer rats were.

'You can't fight like this,' shouted Satan, 'this is war!'

'No, no, no, dude,' replied a swaying M.C. 'This is *Queen*!'

Then Alison raised her arm and took over, singing: 'We will, we will, sock you – sock you!'

The guardians echoed, pulling faces and pointing disdainfully directly at Satan.

'We will, we will, sock you – sock you!'

Satan was livid – how dare they mock HIM – the ruler of Corliol! 'Finish them!' he screamed.

But before he had finished the command, a bolt of grapefruit hit him square in the nose and he could do nothing else but frantically use both paws to flick the offensive eye-smarting fruit away.

Ben and Sam gave William a thumbs up, *He always was a Sourpuss!* mouthed William.

#

At the entrance, the knights had the cats in disarray, until the unthinkable happened: a Rusty Spot caught Hannibal's back wheel with her tail. Hannibal hit the floor, trapping his leg beneath the bike but throwing Flower clear: well, clear into a pillar!

The knights pulled up in shock, the cats turned to pounce, but just as all seemed lost, a gruff voice sounded from the main door: it was Gripper!

'Here kitty kitty,' she bellowed mockingly into the tricycle's ghetto blaster fixed to her back.

The cats looked her up and down – *one more knight wouldn't make much difference* – then turned back to devour Hannibal, who was lying stunned next to one of the brass lifts.

Suddenly there was a roar and as the felines turned to recheck the lone Knight they had so quickly dismissed, their eyes opened wide in terror. Thundering towards them was no Knight on a bike, but one powering a large hamster wheel, showering dynamice everywhere.

The cats scattered in panic.

Nudged by Peter, Robbie dived forward, scooped up Hannibal and Flower and dashed down the steps to the crypt.

Gripper was amazing. As she reached the far side of the Cathedral, she cleverly tilted the wheel to the left and deftly made it arc through the Regimental Chapel and back towards the main door. Bars and Pox weaved in and out behind her, frustrating the feline attacks, as Greaser and Scar (the pillions) scattered the floor with dynamice, slowing the cats down, before they escorted her outside.

#

Luci managed to call several of the pride back to reinforce Satan and her bodyguards. When they drew near, she could see they were in a sorry state: eyes watering, nostrils burning, and constantly picking at the gooey citrus sweets and tarts clinging to their fur. She ushered them through the arch to her king.

On noticing, Satan gestured them forward. 'Enough is enough!' he exclaimed, and, losing his cool, he marshalled the larger cats together and led a charge at the base of the rodent pyramid.

The guardians lost their nerve, and scattered, toppling those above them, who jumped and somersaulted in panic, simultaneously squeezing to safety under the choirstalls.

The exception was Alison, who somehow had kept hold of her guitar as she fell. She knew there was no time and just stood there, resigned to her fate, eyes screwed shut: awaiting the rip of the claw or the crunch of the jaw.

Satan leapt victoriously, his mouth opening in mid-flight ready to receive his treat.

#

In the split-second before he made contact, Harry swooped down, grabbed Alison and, pedalling furiously, swept her up.

Unable to change direction, Satan's head, lips, teeth, slammed into the solid woodwork – *scrunch*! He let out a haunting cry, and even Robbie couldn't help covering his own mouth as he imagined the pain.

Satan got to his feet, shaking as much out of anger as pain, blood seeping from his lips, accompanied by several of his front teeth.

'Shine a light!' grimaced Robbie, almost in sympathy.

It was then the clock struck one.

#

Satan roused himself immediately, and motioned to Yak and Uza, calling '*Qu-ith*, the bowl!' But they, and all the cats nearby, just stared at their mighty ruler, sporting not only a distasteful lip but an hilarious lisp. M.C. of course, couldn't contain himself and guffawed out loud, till Satan caught his eye, and displayed his fury.

'The bowl!' Satan insisted, completely unaware of the other's merriment.

Yak and Uza finally rushed forward, lips tightly closed (to disguise their snickering), offering the bowl with its mirror facing up. The stars began opening, rocketing their planets into the sky.

'No, No!' Marcus called to them, 'Go back, go back, it's not safe!'

But the celestial beings couldn't or wouldn't listen; they were so enjoying themselves, they seemed oblivious to the danger. A planet, mesmerised by the reflection of a possible twin, zoomed down into the bowl. Another did the same.

'No, NO!' cried Peter, 'Look! The others are joining it!'

Soon six or seven planets were happily ensconced in the bowl.

'I think there's only one to go!' Peter gasped, just as, to his horror, it joined them.

'*Exthellent*,' exclaimed Satan.

'No, no, no!' screamed Robbie, and recklessly sprinted forward. But just as Uza had managed to seal the lid… his leg was taken away from beneath him by half a kilogram of mega-mouse, crashing into his shin.

To Uza's horror, the bowl shot up towards the ceiling, and almost in slow motion, all watched its path with open mouths and eyes, as it traced an arc through the air.

Yak leapt after it but missed. Uza dived, but again the bowl only brushed his fingertips.

'Yes!' Robbie shouted, hurtling forward, 'Let it smash!'

But just before it hit the stone floor, Satan threw himself onto his back and slid directly beneath it, paws open.

Robbie was but feet away – but too far to stop him.

'Finally,' Satan purred, as the sealed bowl floated down towards his greedy embrace.

But as it landed in his grasp, Robbie flung himself forward, landing with a thump, not just on Satan's stomach, but on the bowl too.

Satan again wailed in pain, and poor Robbie did too: he felt like someone had just kneed him in the stomach. He crouched, gripping his tummy, struggling to breathe.

Maximus stood up a bit dazed, but Marcus signalled to Ben and Sam to snatch the bowl.

Satan rolled onto his front in agony, and Yak and Uza began helping him to stand. He brushed them aside, called to M.C. and Hunter, and breathlessly commanded 'Spifflicate them!'

M.C. blundered forward swiping Ben and Sam aside, leaving Marcus standing alone, his back to the glass, his arms spread as if trying to hide it. He began to shake as he saw a drooling leopard-like cat licking its lips and leaning back on its haunches…

'Angels and ministers of grace defend us!' he gasped.

…but the beast had already sprung into the air.

CHAPTER 20 — A STAR IS TORN

Hunter swooped down like an eagle, with deadly precision; the second before he struck, he could clearly distinguish Marcus's arms trying to shield his head. The futile gesture almost made him smile. His talons and teeth mercilessly struck…

…Hunter had no idea! Crunch!

It was certainly wooden, certainly solid, and certainly not the soft, sumptuous flesh of a mouse! Hunter shook his head, dazed eyes opened, as before him stood two Temple shields, braced by two Temple angels. More hovered down from the ceiling, forming an impenetrable wall, with Marcus and the bowl cowering beyond it.

Hunter staggered back humiliated and embarrassed as much as flabbergasted. In all the years they had known him, the pride had never seen him so vulnerable and weak.

Satan made no move to comfort him, just smirked callously at his rival's exposure, then turned back to business. 'Attack!' Satan yelled, and the newly strengthened cats galloped forward hurtling into the shields one after the other.

'Hold!' shouted the front angel – and they did!

'Again!' commanded Satan, and this time, they banded together, and all struck simultaneously.

The angels were forced back, but only by a few centimetres.

William, with Ben, Sam and several of the guardians, then emerged from under the kneelers.

'Loose!' he called, and a volley of lemon juice, lime tarts and grapefruit bolts rained down on the hapless attackers: who shielded their watering eyes and frantically began prizing the tarts from their fur. Sam shot out on his skateboard, and skilfully circled the assailants, slinging grapefruit pieces into their faces, before skidding back into his companions' lines. The Guardians then took shelter to reload.

Worryingly Satan didn't seem too disturbed, he just waited for his troops to recover.

'He's up to something!' warned Robbie, feeling much more himself. 'Where the heck are the knights?'

'They'll be back,' assured Hannibal, 'they'll just be re-arming.'

Satan simply held his ground, then clicked his paws three times.

And THEN they saw it.

A bunch of kitten-sized, turban-capped cats came into view, pushing two large catapults, towing two large carts of porridge.

Satan stared into the angels' eyes and pronounced slowly and deliberately: 'THIS WILL NOT END WELL FOR YOU,' then added, 'I *WILL* have my star.'

Gabriel and Raphael, the two lead angels, glanced at each other, but neither flinched nor answered.

'Very well,' continued Satan and nonchalantly clicked his fingers again. An enormous wodge of porridge flew through the air and exploded on their raised shields.

'Tortoise!' called Gabriel, and the angels immediately formed the *testudo* – a Roman battle formation where shields are placed above as well as in front, to repel an aerial attack.

Seven, eight, ten cats then charged forward pushing them back. 'Hold!' But the angels slipped back even further. The *flumph* of the catapults echoed around the cathedral and the porridge continued to rain down shot after shot. It was clear that several of the angel squad were beginning to stiffen, their shields cracking under the weight of the clarty lumps.

'We've got to help!' Robbie gasped. So, accompanied by Peter, Hannibal and Flower, they crawled along the canons' stalls, out of sight and took up position behind Hamish, whose wings had already been paralysed by the initial shelling. Robbie slipped off his jacket and spread it over him.

'Och, thank ye,' he responded in surprise.

'We can't hold them much longer,' whispered Raphael.

#

The stars and planets continued circling and shooting around the building, apparently unaware of the danger they were in.

Then, belatedly, the solution came to Robbie: 'Just unscrew the lid!' he shouted.

'I've been trying,' answered Marcus, 'it's too wide for us, even Maximus can't get a grip.'

It's now or never, accepted Robbie, and crawled forward, handing off *splodges* of porridge in an attempt to shield his compatriots who followed.

Then Gabriel suddenly raised his arm – and Satan, seeing it, did the same; and the shelling ceased.

Robbie took the opportunity to weave to the centre to reach Marcus and the bowl.

'Finally,' sighed Satan, 'of course I'll accept your surrender, just hand me the bowl.'

Quickly Robbie went to twist the lid – but it wouldn't move – it was firmly seized.

'Smash it!' gruffed Hannibal.

'No!' reasoned Marcus, 'we can't have any of the planets damaged!'

'I think it's the porridge,' Robbie suggested, wiping as much off the lid as he could.

Suddenly they were shunted backwards, and two angels fell onto them, one catching Robbie above his eyebrow with his crumbling shield.

'Sugar, Honey…,' Robbie howled, he'd never felt such a cold, deep, pain. His eyes began to flood, his chest began to sob, and he was convinced his skull had caved in. He let out a paralysing shriek. The squeal was so high, so intense, so continual, that, as his dad would have warned: *it will mess with your brain, you know.* And he was right.

Peter, Hannibal, all the guardians covered their ears: but the cats… literally froze. Satan, M.C. and Hunter seized their ears to try and block the pain. The whole pride did the same. It went through them like an earthquake – leaving them shaking and swaying and so unsteady on their feet that many were falling over. Satan himself collided with a catapult, then fell backwards, into one of the porridge carts – his legs akimbo, protruding comically.

Robbie, incredibly, sang on!

When he finally stopped, the felines simply looked relieved and several, with their coats matted with dynamice, their eyes stinging with lemon juice, their ears painfully ringing, began to leave.

‘We’ve done it!’ smiled Marcus, and a whisper of relief rippled through the Temple.

Then suddenly, from the depths of a cart, a cat-like shape arose, scooped the offending oats from its eyes and nose in disgust and stood defiantly. It then raised an arm and aggressively pointed at Robbie.

‘This is the end!’ it announced, ‘Surrender or die!’

Robbie smiled. ‘I’ll… I’ll sing again!’ he threatened.

Satan climbed out of the cart and called his pride to him.

‘What’s he up to?’ whispered Peter.

‘Action stations!’ called Hannibal: and William began mustering his guardians for another volley. Gabriel and Raphael picked up their shields and braced themselves; but the others, though managing to brush off most of the porridge on their armour, were unable to save their disintegrating defences. Nevertheless, they re-formed their scrum.

Robbie again tried to work the lid, but now that his hands were smeared with porridge, it was harder than ever.

All twenty or so felines emerged from their huddle, looking surprisingly confident. They formed into a triangle formation behind Satan, like an R.A.F. display team, and the angels melded into a similar shape behind their surviving shields.

‘I WILL sing again!’ warned Robbie.

Satan strained forward ‘*Thing* again?’ then smiled, ‘Go ahead boy!’

Robbie stood and let rip. The cats, screwed up their faces, and Satan began to shake and wobble as before – but then suddenly stopped, even though Robbie sang on.

‘Look at their ears! Look at their ears!’ panicked Peter. And sure enough, each feline had grey plugs of porridge blocking them.

‘Great Tolfink!’ gasped Marcus.

Robbie stopped. Satan raised his arms above his head and started clapping sarcastically.

‘Is that all you have?’ he mocked: ‘*I’th* unpleasant, but not *incapathitating*,’ he gloated (but to several audible giggles behind him).

Robbie’s inner voice told him it was over. *Was this it?* he wondered, *Have we got this far for nothing?*

Satan waved his pride forward.

Then suddenly, a small motorbike headlight came through the organ arch behind them. Then another.

‘The knights are back!’ clapped Peter excitedly.

Satan pointed to the Dragon Li and ginger toms. ‘You’ve *th’een* them off *one’th*, *ju’th* hold them for a while – it won’t take *u’th* long.’

M.C. now shook with laughter.

But just as they were about to pounce something unexpected happened. Another headlight appeared, followed by two more.

Satan looked at Hunter, who simply shrugged in puzzlement.

And it didn’t stop there. Rider after rider pulled up behind the knights creating a whole traffic jam of miniature bikes – with the sound of even more approaching outside.

‘Boss! Boss!’ M.C. choked, ‘There’s loads of them!’

‘*Impo’thible*!’ cried Satan, ‘they *mu’th* have every knight in the Borders!’

With undisguised panic in his eyes, Satan tried to save face. 'If only I had my full pride!' he sighed. Then called to his cats: 'The Fire Escape, now!' pointing down the side aisle to his owner's Vestry. There was a mad scramble to the doorway and even Hunter bolted. Satan though shook his paw at Robbie menacingly and bared his teeth (which now looked more comical than threatening), hissing triumphantly, *'Ha'tha la V'ithla!',* which elicited guffaws rather than dread from those around him.

#

The guardians crept out of the various niches where they had been hiding. It took a few minutes for the merriment to subside. The Knights of Lonercost cruised up the aisle.

Marcus turned to Hannibal: 'I can't thank you enough. Where on earth did you find so many knights?'

'*Nowt* to do with me,' shrugged Hannibal.

Then, the thirty or forty reinforcements came into view: and to everyone's horror, they were not on motorbikes but mopeds, they wore no armour but bright blue helmets and luminous jackets.

'Sorry *marra,*' the lead rider explained, 'Pizza Domine. Which one of you is Jan?'

There was a moment of consternation, then mouse after mouse completely lost it – the whole building echoing with howls and hoots, some happily rolling on the stone cold floor.

Peter struggled to speak, but finally stuttered: 'Wait… until he finds out… his pride was defeated… by… by… pizza delivery mice!'

Jan interjected, adding a note of seriousness: 'But I haven't ordered any pizzas!'

'I'm sure we can use them,' resolved Marcus. 'Gaston can have the night off and we've all missed supper. Don't worry Jan, the community will pay.'

Just then three miniature Harley Dovidsons roared through the mopeds.

'Here are my knights!' announced Hannibal. Bars and Pox (with Scar and Greaser riding pillion) and Gripper now on the trike, were looking around them, in puzzlement.

Even Robbie, with a banging head and bruised stomach began to smile.

Alison began to sing. 'We will, we will, sock you, sock you!'

The company were soon clapping and stamping the beat, singing along.

Marcus went over to Robbie, 'You, sir, were brilliant!' Then scrambling up to his shoulder, whispered: 'And if you don't mind me asking, which Stellarii are you?'

Robbie's whole being detonated with pride. The warmth spread from his feet to his cheeks. He thought for a moment, then replied: 'Oh, THAT would be telling!'

Marcus nodded knowingly, 'My apologies. You're obviously one of their most experienced agents.' The Prior then scampered down, whispered something to Maximus, who nodded and slipped out, then Marcus called everyone together, 'This merits a feast!' he proclaimed, beckoning the pizza-delivery mice to draw near.

But as all moved forward, one sacrimouse turned to leave, his shoulders hunched, his head hung low. Marcus though spotted him.

'Peter! Peter! Where are you going?' he shouted, running after him and gathering him in a warm embrace. 'It's so good you're alive!'

But Peter tore himself away, fell on his knees and began to weep.

'It's all my fault. Brothers, sisters,' he called out, 'it's all my fault – please forgive me, I don't deserve to be a guardian anymore – but I beg you, let me stay – and I'll willingly be a servant to you all.'

Silence fell across the building.

Marcus placed his hand on Peter's shoulder. 'Our dearest Peter,' he whispered, 'being a guardian is not a reward that can be earned, it is only a gift that can be accepted. And that gift still stands.'

Slowly Peter raised his head to see the welcoming smile on Marcus' face.

'Now come,' concluded The Prior, 'let's not waste these wonderful pizzas; come gather round! You too!' He beckoned to the delivery mice, 'All are welcome at the Maker's table. Paul, Molly, would you please bring the goblets?'

Knights, angels, guardians, and the Pizza Domine riders all closed in around him.

'Oh,' Marcus added, to Will, Ben and Sam, 'I wonder if we might share in some of your non-existent fermentation?'

They all looked rather sheepish.

'Ah,' grimaced William, 'we might be able to provide some, but we heard there was a little accident with the main supply tonight.'

'Accident?' Marcus asked, then closed his eyes, raised his paw in a 'stop' gesture and advised, 'I really don't need to know. But I'm sure you have more stashed away somewhere?'

William and the twins glanced at each other then shook their heads sorrowfully.

'Oh, come now,' Marcus challenged, 'there must be more?'

'Nope. Sorry,' answered William.

'Really?' Then Marcus leant over and whispered, 'I would try behind the pan cupboard in the kitchen if I were you.'

William, Ben and Sam stepped back in horror. 'How long have you…?'

'Just bring it will you?' Marcus prompted, 'The whole crate if you please!'

The three culprits smiled and scampered off.

'I think I have a bottle,' admitted Jan.

'Er, *moi aussi*,' added Gustav, and then Alison, and then Robinson said the same, and to everyone's surprise, Petunia stepped forward and offered five!

'Medicinal purposes,' she explained.

Within half an hour, all were seated on the cushions along the altar rail enjoying four cheese pizzas quaffed with gallons of Dandelion and Burdock. Even Robbie had a taste – though it was only like eating mini crackers to him!

Suddenly a cheer erupted as none other than Edmund came running down the aisle, followed by a grumpy-looking Jan.

Marcus stood, 'Edmund is it really you?'

''Fraid so,' interrupted Jan 'he's been trapped in my room – and…'

'The source of the pizzas!' completed the Prior, grinning.

'I was only trying to get a message out,' excused Edmund.

'Everything's fine,' assured Marcus 'it's just good to have you back.'

The company broke out into song again: even Robbie joined in. Then Marcus stood and held up his hand, and respectfully all fell silent.

'A toast,' he announced, 'to our angels, our knights, and all you brave guardians. But,' he looked up at Robbie, 'especially to our Stellarii, who put his life on the line several times tonight, and without whom we would never have won the victory.'

The gathering broke out into cheers and whooping, Robbie broke out in an embarrassed rash.

'And in token of his self-sacrifice and bravery… Maximus?' The oversized mouse appeared carrying a credit card sized package. 'On behalf of us all, and our wonderful Maker, we'd like you to accept this small token of our thanks.'

Robbie didn't know how to respond, but carefully bent down to receive his gift to more applause and cheers.

'Go on, unwrap it!' shouted Jan, smiling.

Robbie easily picked off the plain brown paper, and there beneath, was a beautiful image of the starlight ceiling. 'Wow,' he grinned, almost unaware of all the high-pitch whooping, and paws banging on the rails and stamping of feet.

'It's the Exchange!' continued Jan.

‘A picture of the Exchange?’ Robbie nodded, in excitement – but Jan unexpectedly threw her head into her hands.

‘It’s not a picture!’ She explained, ‘It IS the Exchange! If you *still* yourself, look into it, let the wonder of the stars touch your heart and calm your breathing, the Maker’s song will grow within you; you’ll become a channel just like us!’

Robbie was stunned. *Not only a Stellarii but a channel for the Exchange, the Maker’s image within me?* It was then his stomach rumbled. *Ooh.* Then another sharp pain. And he realised how late it was into the night – early morning really.

‘Thanks everyone,’ he interrupted, ‘but I must be going now.’

The partying mice waved goodbye, but Jan again drew near. ‘See you soon?’

‘Absolutely!’ Robbie replied. *I’m a Stellarii! A Stellarii!* He beamed, as he retrieved his jacket and half-skipped, half-limped, through the organ arch.

#

When he stepped outside, he locked his fingers together and raised his arms in a stretch. *Ow!* – He’d forgotten his stomach again. He rubbed it gently, yawned, then turned to go home.

But as he as he glanced up at the gates, in the light of a streetlamp he caught sight of a shadowy figure passing Vernon’s lodge: a large golden cat, holding…

…a glass bowl sparkling like a jar of glow worms.

‘Planets!’ he screamed, ‘Luci!’

He squealed – and broke out into a run. By the time he reached the street, there was no sign of her. He dashed into the city – nothing. He doubled-back towards the river – nothing.

Robbie froze, in both senses of the word. First, he could not move. Second, an icy chill invaded his body dismissing his thick camouflage jacket and combat trousers. He just stood there, gulping short, sharp, breaths. His stomach twisted tortuously; his legs wobbled rhythmically, and his lungs burned as if at the end of a cross-country run. In desperation he gripped his thumping chest, then rushed his trembling hands to cushion his exploding temples: but it was all in vain. He had nothing more to give. *Was this dying?*

Sinking to his knees on the cold stone pavement, he closed his flooding eyes. Why had he ever agreed to get involved? Why couldn't he have said no? Why hadn't he noticed her? It was all his fault. He let rip with a terrifying shriek.

The note was so high, so intense, the starlings in the trees, then the gulls on the rooftops, blasted into the air in sequence – like a firework display. The inaudible sound so permeated the thick cathedral walls that the guardians immediately ceased their song and flooded out, in anxiety.

Jan spotted him first and galloped towards him. 'Robbie! Robbie!' she screamed, climbing onto his knee, 'Are you ok?'

Robbie fell silent. The guardians, the Knights flooded around him.

'She's got a star!' Robbie wept. 'Luci, she's got a star!'

Marcus mouthed 'Go and check, will you?' to Lesley, who rushed back into the cathedral.

'It's all my fault!' Robbie sobbed, 'I should have said, they had TWO bowls!'

The guardians turned to each other in shock, some mumbling but most just shaking their heads slowly in disbelief.

Lesley reappeared but was walking much slower and her staunch, taut, face – said it all.

Robbie wiped his eyes. He took a deep sobbing breath, picked himself up, and brushing Jan and the others aside, trudged off robotically towards the castle. To them, he was simply in a street. To him, he was in that classroom again, drowning in darkness and emptiness; only this time, he was not in deep space, but a black hole.

'Robbie wait!' shouted Jan, 'We'll get it back! We'll find a way. Wait, please!'

But he wouldn't, couldn't.

CHAPTER 21 — A STAR IS BORN

As morning came, Robbie awoke from a restless sleep, grabbed his dressing gown and plodded downstairs. He sat at the kitchen table, and just stared into his chocobix.

He was really hungry but couldn't bear to eat. Though he remembered Jan had assured him they'd find a way of getting it back, he knew the chances were miniscule. His one chance, his only chance, had ended in disaster. His inner voice convinced him it was over. *Call yourself a Stellarii?* it mocked. *You couldn't even stop Luci! You're useless. They'll never want YOU back!*

He turned on the T.V. They were showing shelves of porridge, then lemon and limes, announcing that the inexplicable shortages were over.

There was then some video of the Cathedral, with Vernon, on his knees trying to clean up what they called 'an unprecedented act of vandalism'. Then a quick shot of his cat, missing several tufts of hair that had to be cut out by a vet.

But most shocking of all, they showed a confused Mr. Armstrong being led from his home by a policeman, and several RSPCA officers, trying to herd a dozen or so cats into their vans (after they had been discovered locked in his summerhouse).

Robbie knew he just had to move on. No-one would believe him at school even if he tried to explain what had happened, not even Catherine! And last night, his dad had grounded him for a whole month! A whole month! – *Unless, unless,* he plotted mischievously, *I might be able to remember that chant?*

He emptied his bowl into the sink, rinsed it, and laid it out to drain; then went back to his bedroom, dejected. He slumped down at the window and picked up the starlight ceiling image that now sat next to his singing trophy; but the stars were no longer alive.

With nothing else to do he set up his telescope and peered into the trees across the back street. *Nothing, not even a pigeon or squirrel!* he groaned. He scanned past the telegraph pole to the lamppost – then had to track back – his heart suddenly jumping to life.

There, at the bottom, where the pole met the pavement, were a couple of small plastic yoghurt bottles filled with black liquid! He focused in on the label and slowly read aloud:

'W.B.S.'s Explosive Dandelion and Burdock, always keep away from children.'

Robbie didn't smile – he roared out loud, 'Yes! Yes! Yes!' Then had to grab his stomach as the bruises stabbed in his tummy. His inner voice, however, passed sentence on his failure: *That was kind of them – but you've got to accept they won't want you back? It's just the kindest way they could think of saying goodbye.*

Robbie's shoulders sank. But then he saw something else below the label – some scribbling, in black marker pen. He focused in and read aloud:

'*Meet...me...tonight...Temple...1am.... Jan.*'

His heart jumped, his arms raised, his hands clasped together in elation as he literally jumped for joy. Maybe there really IS a star in every black hole! He dreamed.

His days as a Stellarii had only just begun!

The End

Cumbrian Dialect Glossary:

Gadgee (man, bloke)

Yan, Tyan, Tethera, Methera, Pimp (one, two, three. four, five.)

Ratching (rummaging)

Foily (smelly)

Keaties (cats)

About the author

Michael was born in Barrow-in-Furness, Cumbria, (at the time, Lancashire) – so he describes himself as a 'Lancumbrian' or 'Cumcastrian'! His earliest memories are: running up and down the terraced streets of Hindpool shooting cowboys with his toy cap gun; watching a submarine being launched from Jubilee Bridge at Vickerstown; days out on the swings and pebbles of Biggar Bank, Walney; and standing on the climbing frame at St. James Infant School.

Though a cautious lad; when his family emigrated to Australia, a whole new world opened up for him. A six-week voyage half-way around the world, brought his first meeting with armed police in Lisbon; camels and crocodiles along the Suez Canal; machine-gunners in Aden; and the natural darkness of the ocean skies festooned with stars; which all fed his vivid imagination and love of storytelling.

From that time, his imagination grew rather than diminished.

On his return to England, less than three years later, though technically homeless, his family were offered accommodation, through the kindness of distant relatives, 'The Kitchings', in Blackburn, Lancashire, where they soon settled.

Though never a lover of reading, at school, Michael excelled in creative writing and dabbled in acting, winning small parts in a variety of productions from *Macbeth* to *Oliver!*

University, a two-year Internship in London, (including a placement in Northern Ireland during *The Troubles*), followed by two years post-graduate training for his profession, led to his first job in Accrington (overlooking the original Stanley football ground!) Jobs in Deepdale, Preston, Central Blackpool, and finally Carlisle followed.

Though a father of three now adult boys, Michael still finds working with children and young people engaging, and is often found leading assemblies in schools, running children's events or providing 'Quiet Days' for adults.

Michael is a firm believer in the power of genuine love, and taking 'time out' to rest, dream, and connect with *The Maker*: 'the one in whom we live, and move, and have our being'.

Whilst working through a recent difficult time in his life, he found talking with friends and family a lifeline, and decided to write a children's fantasy story, simply for fun.

Four years later, it became the book you hold today.

Printed in Great Britain
by Amazon